D1497837

THE HAUNTING OF GREY HILLS
Tyger, Tyger

JENNIFER SKOGEN

EPIC
Press

Tyger, Tyger
The Haunting of Grey Hills: Book #6

Written by Jennifer Skogen

Copyright © 2016 by Abdo Consulting Group, Inc.

Published by EPIC Press™
PO Box 398166
Minneapolis, MN 55439

Cover design by Dorothy Toth
Images for cover art obtained from iStockPhoto.com
Edited by Melanie Austin

LIBRARY OF CONGRESS CATALOGING-IN-PUBLICATION DATA

Skogen, Jennifer.
Tyger, Tyger / Jennifer Skogen.
p. cm. — (The haunting of Grey Hills ; #6)
Summary: A final choice must be made that could change the world forever. Each
person must answer one final question: what am I willing to do for the people I love?
And what does death even mean, in a world full of ghosts?
ISBN 978-1-68076-034-7 (hardcover)
1. Ghosts—Fiction. 2. High schools—Fiction. 3. Supernatural—Fiction.
4. Haunted places—Fiction. 5. Young adult fiction. I. Title.
[Fic]—dc23
2015932723

EPICPRESS.COM

To the city of Port Townsend: all the atmosphere of Grey Hills . . . but fewer ghosts

Prologue

Mabel was supposed to love him.

After all, Eli Grey loved her. Eli thought about her all the time. She was the memory of a beautiful song that wove in and out of his dreams. She was a splinter that had been driven so deep beneath his skin that it had healed over. She was a part of him.

Wasn't that what love did to you—changed you? Made you into something new? Something better?

He used to watch Mabel when she walked from her parents' shop to the Opal Theater, where she sold cigarettes and candy. Some days she would hurry through the summer rain. Mabel was most beautiful then—her damp hair curling around her face, mud spattering the hem of her dress and her leather boots. She looked so alive.

Occasionally Eli would follow her into the Opal. He would buy a penny bag of licorice, and Mabel would smile when he pressed the coin into the palm of her hand. As he watched the film, Eli imagined the music from the piano drifting out to the lobby. He pictured each note brushing her face and entwining around the fingers of her delicate hands.

Even though the Opal almost exclusively played films, a local theatrical company still put on one play every season. That summer it was *Hamlet*. Mabel played the tragic Ophelia, and Eli himself donated the roses that decorated her hair. He cut them from his brother's garden.

Mabel died beautifully.

Chapter 1

"Don't turn around," said a man's voice. "I have a gun pointed at your head."

Dom tightened his grip on the flashlight. He started to reach toward the handle of the shovel with his other hand when a girl's voice said, "How about you don't move at all, okay? In fact, just put your hands up while you're at it."

"Who are you?" Dom asked, trying to keep his voice steady. He raised his hands, while maintaining a firm hold on the flashlight. A beam of light shot up into the branches of the poplar tree.

Rain dripped into his eyes, and Dom wanted to reach up and wipe it away but he also didn't want his head to end up with a big hole in it like poor Mabel's. At the thought of bullets, Dom's shoulder began to pulse with a deeper, red ache.

"You're Dominick, right?" the guy asked, not answering Dom's question. "Dominick Vega?"

"Pleased to meet you," Dom said. "I'd shake your hand, but, you know . . . hard to do with your hands in the air."

"Funny," said the girl. "Gregory didn't tell us you were funny." Her high-pitched voice sounded young—maybe even younger than Dom—but it was hard to tell by voice alone.

At Gregory's name, Dom's head fell forward. Rain dripped down the back of his neck. He heard Sam's voice in his head: *Fucking Gregory.*

Dom knew that things between Trev and Gregory had ended badly, but Dom hadn't thought that there might be a legitimate reason why Trev hated his ex. That was just what people did—break up and get all pissy about it.

What hadn't Trev told them about Gregory?

For that matter, how much did Dom even know about their old friend, except that Gregory had swept into their lives with an almost staggering suddenness? No, Dom reasoned with himself. If these people knew Gregory, then they must be here to help.

But why were they pointing a gun at him?

"Gregory sent you, huh?" Dom said. "So you must be the backup he was talking about."

"I like that," the guy said with a small laugh. "Yeah, we're the *backup*."

"We're not just *backup*," clarified the girl. "We're the guys who ride in on white horses and save your ass. We're the fucking cavalry."

"And why, exactly," Dom asked, "does the cavalry have a gun pointed at my head? Did Gregory forget to mention that we're on the same fucking side?" Dom's legs were tired from holding his rather awkwardly perched position over the coffin, and his shoulder was moving from a low-level throb to a sharper pain. It was starting to feel like someone was jabbing his bullet wound with the tip of their finger.

"And what side is that, Dominick Vega?" asked the girl. It was unnerving to not be able to see the people talking to him. He tried to imagine what they looked like, but could only picture the metallic glint of the gun the man must be holding.

"Um," Dom said, "The side that fights ghosts?"

The man laughed, but the girl didn't. She said, "You know almost nothing about the war we're fighting. But that's okay. We'll teach you."

"Thanks," said Dom. "I can see you're the charming one."

Dom really wanted to put his arms down, but when he started to lower them the guy spoke up again. "Hey now, keep those up."

Dom sighed and raised his arms a little higher.

"Okay, Dominick—" continued the girl.

"You can call me Dom."

She paused. "What?" she asked in a very incredulous tone.

"People call me Dom—Dominick is too long."

"Do you think I'm too dumb to remember three syllables?"

Dom shrugged, but realized it might be too dark for them to notice. It also really hurt his shoulder.

"Okay, Dominick," she said. "Let's get you out of that hole."

Slowly, Dom turned around. He looked up and saw two dark figures standing over him. It was hard to see their features, but the man looked older—maybe late twenties? He bent down to offer Dom a hand.

"Here," the man said. Dom took his hand with his good arm, and let the man pull him out of the grave. "I'm Collins, by the way. This is Julia."

"Is Collins a first or a last name?" Dom asked, hardly paying attention to what he was saying. All he could think about was the pain in his shoulder, which had just been wrenched again during the scramble out of the grave. He wanted another pill.

Collins grinned. "First, I guess. Doesn't matter—it's not my real name."

The girl had a hood pulled up over her face. Dom had a flash of Macy in her Halloween costume, with the red hood of her cape covering her forehead.

He banished the memory and focused on the girl in front of him. *Julia.* Who, it turned out, was actually the one with the gun.

"Why did you dig up this grave?" Julia asked. Her grip on the gun was steady, but she didn't seem to be threatening him with it. It was more like a reminder of how it could stand between them if he misbehaved.

"You don't know?" Dom asked. "I thought you knew everything."

Dom held the flashlight just behind his back. He tried to be casual about it, hoping the other two would forget that he had what amounted to a short, electric club in his hand. Or maybe they had never noticed.

"We know that you received a phone call, and then you left the house. We know that Trevor and Gregory are looking for Matilda—you call her Sam now, don't you? We know that *Sam* is harboring a dangerous ghost. And, most importantly, we know that we can help you."

"I can't see your face, and you're pointing a gun at me," Dom said, trying to keep his voice light. "To be honest, the vibe I'm getting from you isn't really *helpful*."

Julia seemed to think for a moment, then lowered the gun. She put it back in a holster at her hip. Then she pulled back her hood, letting the rain fall into her face. Julia was standing close enough now that, even in the dark, Dom could see that her hair was streaked with gray, and there were hard lines on the side of her mouth. He had thought she was a lot younger.

Collins stepped closer too. He was tall and broad—he had to be strong to have so easily pulled Dom out of the grave. His leather jacket seemed a little impractical in the slushy rain. Julia's raincoat was a better idea.

"Do you need to sniff our butts, too?" Collins asked. When Julia gave him a sharp look, he explained, "Because that's what dogs do . . . when they meet each other? It was supposed to be a joke."

"If you let me hold the gun I'll laugh at anything you say," Dom said.

"Look," Julia said in an impatient tone, "I'm sorry about the gun. We just didn't know how you were going to react to us."

"How I would react to Gregory's friends? I mean, you could have given me a little credit. I don't usually go around attacking people my friends sent to help me. You could have just started with 'Gregory says hi' or something a little more civil than a gun."

"Duly noted," said Julia.

Then, when Dom thought that they might have forgotten about the whole exhumed skeleton thing, Collins said, almost as if he was talking about the weather, "And why, exactly, were you digging up this grave?"

Dom didn't know why he was so reluctant to share what Sam had told him with these strangers—that Eli's journal was a Token that might be able to save Jackson. If Julia and Collins were really here to help—if Gregory had really sent them—then shouldn't Dom be eager to have someone else on his side? Before they arrived, the only assistance he had gotten that night was from some painkillers and a shovel.

The wind started to pick up, and it lifted Julia's hair from her shoulders. She went to pull her hair back into a ponytail, and Dom noticed that her right hand—the hand that had just been holding the gun—was burned. He shouldn't have been able to see it in the darkness, but there was something about the texture, or the how the faint light of the moon glinted off the scar tissue.

Dom was reminded of Lorna—both from her scars and her gun. He rubbed his shoulder again, wishing that it was time to take another pill. He had started keeping a few of them in an old Altoids tin in his jacket pocket.

He realized he still hadn't answered their question. "We thought something was buried here," Dom said. "Something that could help us destroy the ghost that's inside our friend."

"Your friend Jackson," Julia said. "A high school student, correct? And the prime suspect in the death of Macy Pierce, allegedly." She sounded like a reporter or maybe a lawyer.

"Did Gregory tell you that?" Dom tried to keep his voice steady, but hearing Macy's name was like a punch to the throat.

Julia nodded. "And it's all over the news."

Ever since Macy's body had been found, Dom had been expecting the police to come knocking on his door, but so far no one had come by. He wasn't going to tell the police the truth, of course—because who the fuck would believe that?—but he didn't know how good he'd be at lying.

Dom had been so careful when he dug Macy back up to remove her finger. He wore gloves, and a ski mask so none of his hair would fall out into the grave. Dom wore shoes that he bought at a thrift store and then threw out immediately after. But there still could be a trace of him—and Trev and Sam—from when they buried Macy in the first place. What would he do if the police came to arrest him?

"And what," Collins asked next, "did you think was buried here?"

Dom told the truth, or part of it. "An old girl-friend of the ghost—those are her bones."

"Nothing else?" Julia asked, peering over into the open grave. "How were her bones supposed to help? Were you thinking of making a Token?" She took out a flashlight and shined it into the hole. Dom was pretty sure he saw her curl her lip in disgust. If she wasn't used to looking at dead things then she was in the wrong line of business.

"Yeah," Dom said. He was careful how he said the next few words. "But we aren't sure if it's going to work. We don't have everything we need." Dom thought about Macy's unfinished Token hidden in Sam's room in the yellow house. Why wouldn't it work? What was Dom missing?

Julia turned to him. He was pretty sure that she was smiling. "That was your plan? To try to control him with his girlfriend's bones? Not a completely terrible idea. But how could you be sure the link is strong enough? It would be best to have *his* bones instead of hers. Her blood might have helped, but of course only if she was alive."

Alive. That word struck something deep inside Dom's gut. He felt lightheaded. Hesitantly, he said, "Yeah, can't really get blood out of a skeleton."

"Dead blood doesn't work," Collins added. "It needs to be from someone living." His tone of voice was almost smug—a student showing off in class. Julia gave him a look that Dom thought was disapproving.

"Yeah," Dom went on, taking another step

backward. His hand on the flashlight was growing slick from the rain. "Guess it was a dead end."

Then he turned and ran.

Dom didn't really think they would shoot him, but his heart was still solidly fixed in his throat—thudding almost in time with his steps—until he reached the gate. Then it simply stopped.

The gate was locked. A new-looking padlock held the gate in place.

When he turned around, Julia had the gun fixed on him again. "Why did you run?" she asked. Collins arrived a few steps behind her. He was shaking his head like Dom had disappointed them.

"Why do you keep pointing a gun at me?" Dom asked in response, but Julia didn't say anything more. While they waited, Julia watching Dom and Dom watching the gun, the moon finally broke entirely free of the clouds for a few seconds. It shone down on Julia like a spotlight.

There was something about her face that Dom couldn't quite wrap his mind around. Something kept changing.

Then it hit him—it was her eyes. He shouldn't have been able to see them in the dark, not the actual colors. But he could see them, and, weirder still, they were changing. As he watched, Julia's eyes flickered from blue to green to brown. She blinked, and her eyes were dark again—colorless once more in the moonlight.

"What is that?" Dom asked, not even sure how to ask the question that was filling his mind. What was he seeing? "Your eyes?"

"You're going to learn," Julia said. "We're going to teach you."

Then Collins closed the distance between him and Dom. The larger man took the flashlight out of Dom's hand and wrenched his arm behind his back. Dom cried out in pain as his shoulder twanged angrily.

As they marched Dom out of the graveyard, Dom remembered Mabel's uncovered grave. He wondered if her ghost could feel the rain on her bones. He hoped she could.

Chapter 2

It had been well over an hour and Dom still hadn't called them back.

"Should we just call him again and make sure he understood the directions?" Claire asked. Claire wasn't sure *she* completely understood the directions. Dig up some woman and take a book out of her grave?

On one hand, it was all pretty straightforward, but still . . . Tokens and ghosts? Sam talked about these things like Claire was just supposed to automatically know all her weird ghost hunting lingo when Claire hadn't even wrapped her head around the *ghost* part. *Ghosts are real?* That question kept popping up into her head at random moments, like, when she was in the bathroom or brushing her hair. *Ghosts are actually real?*

Claire plugged in her phone with a charger she bought in the lobby. They had *everything* down there. She almost bought a little "Get Well Soon" teddy bear, but then Claire remembered that she wasn't in a hospital, and Jackson wasn't just sick. He was possessed by a fucking ghost.

Ghosts are real???

Sam started to shake her head *no* to Claire's question, but then she ran a hand through her hair—sort of tugging on the ends. Sam always did that when she was nervous, Claire had noticed over the past few days. "Well, maybe?" Sam said. "It couldn't hurt anything to call Dom, right?"

Claire handed Sam her phone, still attached to the wall by the charger cord. Sam let it ring and ring. There was apparently no answer because Sam muttered, "Shit," and handed the phone back.

More hair-pulling.

"Do you think we should just call Trev?" Claire asked. "Now that you know how to help Jackson, maybe he'll stop trying to kill him?"

"But what if he doesn't?" Sam asked softly.

Claire didn't really have a response for that. She glanced across the room at Jackson where he lay on the bed unconscious. Sam had shot him with another tranquilizer after the whole *ear cutting* thing. If the ghost didn't kill Jackson, those drugs were going to.

Claire suddenly realized that, without Macy, Jackson was probably her best friend. What an unsettling thought . . .

Sorry I pepper-sprayed you. And kicked you in the face. And ran you over with my car. Sorry I can't rip that ghost out of your body and take you to a hospital. That's what Claire imagined doing—just reaching into his chest (or wherever it was that ghosts lived when they camped out inside of a person) and pulling Eli out by his neck.

"You know, let's just wait another hour," Claire

finally said. "Then we'll decide if we should call the others. Let's just take a deep breath, okay? We don't need to do anything yet."

"Okay," Sam said. Her hair was wrapped so tightly around her finger that it looked like it was cutting off the circulation.

"Deep breath," Claire repeated, patting Sam on the head—which was something she never could have imagined herself doing a few days earlier. That's when Claire noticed the blood on her own hand, just below one of her knuckles. It must be Sam's blood, from when Sam had tried to cut her own ear off like a psychopath.

Claire rubbed at the blood. Her stomach did a little butterfly flip.

"I'm gonna take a shower," Claire said, frowning down at her hand. "Get us some food, okay?"

"Yeah, sure." Sam was still staring at the phone.

The shower was blissful. Claire used the shitty hotel shampoo and scoured her hand, scraping at the blood with her fingernails. Everything smelled like oranges and maybe jasmine or some other generic *flower* scent.

All that mattered was that it didn't smell like blood or Jackson's unwashed body. The hotel room was actually becoming quite rank. They should probably open some windows, or maybe she would go back down to the lobby and get some air freshener or a nice smelling candle. *Something* to cut through the stink.

Claire was just thinking how she might just stay in the shower forever when she heard Sam call out something like, "Did you order room service?"

Claire didn't have time to answer before she heard shouting.

Chapter 3

When Trev pushed open the hotel room's door, he noticed two things. First, the rain was so loud that it sounded like it was inside the room. Second, Jackson was stretched out on one of the beds, his hands cuffed to the bed frame.

Jackson looked like he was already dead, which filled Trev with equal parts relief and horror. Even from across the room Trev could see how hollow Jackson's eyes looked, and how sickly his face was. There were bloodstains on his shirt, and Trev didn't know if they were fresh or from the last time he saw Jackson about two days earlier.

Then Trev looked at Sam. There was dried blood on the side of her face.

"Trev?" she said, her face slipping from a smile to a look of shock. Sam put her hand up to her ear, which was, Trev realized, the source of the blood.

"Mattie?" he said, his voice catching in his throat. He didn't care in that moment that his sister hated to be called by her old nickname. "Are you okay?"

Before she could answer, Gregory stepped into the room behind him. He put his hands on Trev's shoulders in a motion that felt so familiar that for a brief second Trev almost stepped back into his arms, but then Gregory moved Trev aside.

"Stay out of the way," Gregory said, and then he pulled a gun Trev hadn't noticed before out of a pocket.

"Hey!" Trev exclaimed, moving between Gregory and his sister. "What the fuck are you doing?"

"Just get back, I'm not going to hurt Sam."

"You didn't tell me you had a gun." Trev's face grew hot. "You can't point a gun at my sister."

Then Claire stepped out of the bathroom. Her hair was dripping, and she was only wearing a towel. One hand was firmly holding the towel in place.

"Claire?" Trev heard himself say. For a moment Trev thought he was hallucinating—that his brain had finally snapped and his insanity was manifesting itself in the form of a short blonde girl.

"Drop the fucking gun," Claire said firmly, "or I'll call 911." Okay, so Claire really was here. And she was pissed.

That's when Trev realized that the sound he had heard wasn't rain. It was the water running from the shower.

"Claire?" Trev said again, remembering all those times he meant to call her over the past two days. "What are you doing here?"

"Who is this?" Gregory said, gesturing toward Claire with his gun.

Claire winced, but didn't move. "My name is Claire, and I'm Jackson's friend. His best friend. And seriously, don't point that thing at me. Do you even know how to use a gun? Are you going to get all trigger happy and accidentally shoot me?"

"Nice to meet you, Claire," Gregory said, "And no, I won't *accidentally* shoot you."

Trev took a step closer to Gregory. "You're not shooting anyone. Just put the gun down."

"And let your sister knock us out again? No way." Gregory was sweating, and he looked . . . wrong somehow. It was his eyes. They were changing colors. Trev thought he had imagined it earlier in the hall, but it was happening again. First, they were dark brown, then a deep blue, then green. Then brown again.

"What did you do?" Trev gasped. He remembered the ghosts Gregory had killed outside of the restaurant. He remembered the ghosts screaming. Whatever Gregory had done to them . . . it must have done something to *him* as well.

Trev grabbed Gregory's arm, but his skin was too hot to touch so he had to let go. "What is happening to you?" Trev said, his voice rising into a shrill plea.

"It doesn't matter anymore," Gregory said, his eyes still flashing different colors. "All that matters is that we stop him."

Then Trev heard someone laughing. He looked past Sam's stricken face to where Jackson was lying on the bed. Jackson was watching them, his lips pulled back into a sneer of delight. He laughed again, and then said, "Thank you."

Jackson's voice was terrible—it was like listening to glass scraping across cement. Trev wanted to cover his ears.

Sam turned toward Jackson. "He shouldn't be awake yet. I just gave him more of the tranquilizer."

Jackson laughed again. "You are all so stupid, aren't you?" And then his wrists began to glow.

"What's happening?" Claire said, taking a step back. "Why is Jackson glowing?"

"What did you do?" Sam cried out. "I was so careful! There are no ghosts in here!" She started looking wildly around the room, as though for some kind of a weapon. Or maybe she was looking for a stray ghost.

"It's okay," Gregory said. "I can destroy him." Gregory's own arms were beginning to glow. The metal of his gun turned a faint blue, reflecting the glow from Gregory's arms.

"Should I call the police?" Claire called out. She now had a phone in her free hand.

"No," Trev called back. "Not yet." What could police do against the kind of freaky blue power Trev had already seen shoot out of Jackson's arms? Trev looked back to Jackson, and he saw tiny blue cracks running through the metal of the handcuffs. Then either the handcuffs or the bedframe—or both—snapped, and Jackson sat up, rubbing his now-bare wrists.

Sam's face crumpled, and for a brief moment Trev thought she was going to collapse right there beside the bed.

Then she ran.

Chapter 4

Sam threw herself onto Jackson, wrapping her arms around his thin, bony body. He was already so battered and broken that it seemed like he would just shatter.

"Run!" Sam yelled, and for a brief, harrowing moment she wondered if this was what it felt like to leap onto a live grenade.

"Mattie!" she heard her brother yell, and his voice pierced straight to the center of her—to that place where their childhood played like a movie projected onto the wall of her heart.

She and Trev were running down the hall into their bedroom. They were jumping on the couch, even after their mom yelled that they were ruining the springs. They were sharing Halloween candy, Trev taking the sour worms, and giving Mattie the chocolate kisses.

Sam reached into the movie of her childhood and gathered her memories around herself like armor. She held on to Jackson's writhing body, and screamed, "Run! Now!"

All this time Sam had her eyes closed. She made herself open them, and she saw Eli looking back through Jackson's eyes. He was still smiling.

"Fuck you," she growled. "Get out of Jackson!" she screamed into his face. She was so close. If Dom could just find the journal then they might be able to destroy Eli without killing Jackson. Then all of this—her flight to Seattle, whatever they did to Vice Principal Fitch, and all of the drugs that she kept pumping into Jackson's poor body—everything would be worth it.

Otherwise she should have just let them kill Jackson in their kitchen and been done with it.

She still remembered the look on Jackson's face when he was tied to the kitchen chair. It almost looked like Eli wanted Gregory to go ahead and kill him.

Did Eli want them to kill Jackson? What was Eli planning?

Eli didn't answer her. Instead, he threw himself forward, slamming his head into Sam's face. Sam didn't just see stars—she saw a fucking supernova exploding before her eyes. Then everything was black.

When Sam woke up she thought she was dead. She was slumped on the far side of the bed with her face mostly covered by a blanket. For a moment she didn't know where she was, or why her fingers came away slick with blood when she touched her face. Then she stood up in an icy, sickening panic.

Eli! Where is Eli?

At first she thought the room was empty, but then she saw legs sticking out of the bathroom. Long legs . . . with a pair of dirty Chucks at the end of them.

Sam froze and watched those legs—Jackson's legs—for any sign of motion. Only when they were still for five beats of her heart did Sam realize the bigger question: *Where are the others?*

She crept toward the bathroom and peered around the corner. Jackson was lying on the ground, his head tilted to one side. His face looked a sickly yellowish color under the bathroom light, and his mouth was slightly open.

His eyes were cracked just a little, just enough that he would have been able to see the base of the toilet if he wasn't . . . Sam's breath caught somewhere lower than her lungs. She felt like her stomach was trying to breathe for her.

Dead. That was the word she didn't even want her thoughts to use. He couldn't be dead.

Sam knelt by Jackson's head and pressed two

fingers to his neck. No pulse. She tried again, cradling his head in the crook of her other arm. Still no pulse. Her mind went blank. This wasn't possible. Not after everything she had done to save him. Not after he had fought so hard to save himself.

"No," Sam whispered. Then she said it again, louder, "No!" She put his head back on the floor and crouched over him, placing one hand on top of the other—both above his heart. "Jackson," she whispered fiercely. It was a command.

She pressed down on his chest, just like she had learned when she took a CPR course her freshman year of high school. That time seemed unbearably long ago, and she struggled to remember the details.

Where was she supposed to place her hands? How hard should she press before his ribs cracked? She had never thought she would need to use CPR when she took the class, and now she hated her past self for not paying more attention.

"Goddamn you, Jackson," she whispered as she pressed his chest again and again. "Listen to me." Again, she pressed. Again. "You are not dead. And if you are you had better fucking come back right now."

Then she tilted his head and pressed her lips to his. She breathed into his lungs.

Sam thought she heard something—a soft gurgling sound. Sam leaned close to his mouth, but he still wasn't breathing.

Again, she pumped his heart for him. Over and over she forced his blood to move through his veins. After thirty more chest compressions she cupped his face and pressed her mouth to his a second time. When she breathed into him, she thought of all the words she had left to say to him, and all the heartbeats he should still have.

How many heartbeats in a lifetime? How many breaths?

Then Sam felt something next to her. Someone. She couldn't see anyone else in the small bathroom, but her skin prickled, and she could almost taste a new fragrance in the air, like the scent of shampoo drifting off a person's hair.

Let him go. The words echoed in the back of Sam's mind. She recognized the voice.

"Macy?" Sam whispered to the air. "No." She shook her head, and her tears fell onto Jackson's chest. "Give him back. You can have him later."

Sam was about to start pounding on his chest again when she thought she heard a sound.

A small, almost inaudible groan came from somewhere deep inside Jackson's body. She put her ear right next to his mouth. Sam felt his breath on her cheek, and then she was sobbing. Not bothering to wipe her tears off her face, Sam stood up and backed away from Jackson, giving him space. He was coughing and making a choking, wheezing sound.

Eli. The ghost's name tolled in Sam's mind. Would it be Eli or Jackson who looked at her with Jackson's eyes?

Jackson tried to sit up, but he was too weak to raise his head. "Sam?" he moaned, lifting a hand to his throat. That was when Sam noticed the red marks at his neck. What the fuck had happened while she was knocked out?

"Jackson?" Sam whispered. She took another step back, then hit the edge of the bathroom door. "Are you . . . ?" She wasn't sure how she meant to finish that sentence. Was he okay? Was he really alive? Was he Jackson at all?

"He's gone, Sam," Jackson said in a low, scratchy voice. "Eli's gone." But there was also a lightness to his voice, and when Jackson tried to lift his head again he was smiling. It wasn't Eli's nasty grin—it was that half-smile that always made Sam's heart do an embarrassing pitter-patter.

"Jackson?" she repeated, not trusting her eyes or her ears. Was she just seeing what she wanted to see? Was it a trick? She hadn't decided when someone touched her shoulder.

It was Trev. He had a nasty lump on the side of his head.

"Gregory's gone," her brother said—nearly repeating the words Jackson had just said. Trev's voice was too calm, too still. "He took Claire."

Chapter 5

After Jackson head-butted Sam and flung her off the side of the bed, it all happened so fast. Trev wanted to run to his sister, but he couldn't seem to move. He felt as if he were watching a movie that he couldn't pause or rewind. There was nothing he could do.

Jackson swung himself off the bed and stood up on shaky legs. Then he walked toward Gregory in a pained, stiff sort of gait. Jackson was smiling, with Sam's blood—or maybe his own—dripping down his face.

Gregory pointed the gun at Jackson, but then the metal of the weapon started to glow, and

Gregory dropped it with a cry. Where the gun hit the ground, the fibers on the carpet began to smolder.

But Trev knew that Gregory didn't need a gun to be dangerous. He was his own weapon. Gregory raised his hands. He almost looked like he was motioning for Jackson to stop, but Trev knew from the strange light coming off Gregory's hands that he was focusing his energy on Jackson. No, not Jackson . . . Eli. Gregory was going to burn Eli out of Jackson's body.

Then Jackson threw himself at Gregory, and the light around both of them was so bright that Trev had to look away.

"Gregory!" Trev called out at the same time Claire, from where she was standing by the bathroom door, screamed, "Jackson!"

When the light faded, Trev saw Gregory's hands locked around Jackson's throat, and they fell together, past Claire, and into the bathroom.

Trev didn't know how long it took, but Jackson

didn't put up much of a fight. He heard a few thumps, as though from a head hitting the ground. Then nothing.

When Gregory walked out of the bathroom, he was grinning. He picked up the gun that he had dropped earlier and put it in his back pocket in one careless, fluid motion. "This is so much better!" Gregory said gleefully. He held his hands out in front of him, as though inspecting them.

"Gregory?" Trev said, not comprehending the look on his face. He didn't look like someone who had just killed another person. He looked so fucking pleased with himself.

"He's just as strong as I had hoped," Gregory said, then let out a loud laugh.

Trev stared at Gregory, his heart stumbling. "What happened? Is Jackson . . . ?"

"Is Jackson dead?" Gregory said, turning his strange, stretched smile toward Trev. "I should think so. You know, I wasn't actually sure what would happen if Jackson died on his own, cuffed to that bed. Where would I go? Sam is strong, but was she strong enough? And Claire . . . well, she's just a tiny thing, isn't she?"

Trev's brain wouldn't believe what he was hearing. "Gregory?" he said again, as though his name might anchor Gregory back to reality—make him stop acting so crazy.

Claire, who had been leaning against the wall next to the door, said the word that broke through Trev's stupor: "Eli?"

Gregory turned to her and pointed a finger like it was a gun. "Tiny but clever. Did anyone ever tell you that? You're always one step ahead of them, aren't you, sweetheart?"

Trev started to shake his head. "No," he mouthed, but he didn't know if he had actually spoken. For a moment all he could hear was the rush of his own heart beating in his ears.

"Well, I think I'd better be off," Gregory said glibly. He pulled the gun out again, almost as an afterthought. He tapped the barrel of it against his forehead. "Hmm . . . you know, I think I'd like some company. Claire?" Gregory nodded toward Claire, who now had her back pressed against the wall as though she could sink into it. She was still just wearing that thin towel. "Why don't you come with me. And Trev?"

Trev couldn't speak. He couldn't move.

Gregory kept talking. "If you follow me I'm going to shoot her in the head. And then maybe I'll cut off one of Gregory's ears. Sam taught me that little trick earlier today. Would you still love him if he was a tad lopsided? Maybe I'll take his nose while I'm at it. Would you like that? Would he still look pretty?"

When Gregory walked out the door with Claire, Trev couldn't help it—he followed.

"Stop!" Trev yelled down the hall. "Gregory! You're stronger than him."

Gregory turned around and walked back until he was so close that Trev could have touched his chest. "It's funny," Gregory whispered into Trev's ear, "but in many ways, Jackson was so much stronger. At least he put up more of a fight." Then Gregory slammed the gun into the side of the Trev's head.

<hr />

"He took Claire," Trev said, then told his sister everything. He raised his fingers to the side of his head and felt the bump that was already forming. It was going to be as big as a fucking ostrich egg.

When Gregory hit him, Trev went down but didn't entirely lose consciousness. He lay on the ground and watched Gregory's dark head and Claire's blonde one disappear into an elevator. Then he made himself get up, even though the world tilted, and the ugly pattern on the hallway carpet went all wobbly. Luckily, the door wasn't completely closed, and he had been able to let himself back in Sam's room.

"What do we do?" he asked Sam.

She looked at Trev like he was stupid. "We go find her!"

"But he said he'd kill her," Trev argued. His stomach was a clenched fist, and his head hurt so much that it wasn't even pain anymore. It was a new language.

Then Trev looked helplessly past Sam to where Jackson was still lying prone on the bathroom floor. "What do we do about him?"

"Nothing. I don't know. How about not killing him for starters?" Sam spat. "Can you try that out this time?"

Trev stared at her. Did she not know? "Sam," he said gently, "Gregory killed him."

Sam shook her head and gave him one of her ferocious smiles. "He's not dead."

He looked past her and saw that Jackson's body wasn't entirely still—his chest was rising and falling ever so slightly. "He's not? But Eli said that Jackson was gone . . . "

"I brought him back."

Trev started to laugh a manic, uncontrollable laugh. "You fucking raised the dead, didn't you?" He threw his arms around her and tried to spin her around.

"Stop it." She pushed him off. "I hurt everywhere."

Trev was about to take a closer look at Jackson—see if there was anything else he could do for him—when he remembered Gregory and Claire.

"Eli has Claire, Sam. And he has Gregory." They both already knew this, but Trev had to say the words out loud one more time to even begin to comprehend what it meant.

They left the Do Not Disturb sign on the door when they went out into the hall. Trev reached for Sam's hand as they walked toward the elevator, and she didn't pull away. Her hand was sticky, and when he realized it was from blood he squeezed her hand tighter. She squeezed it back. He thought he could feel one or both of their heartbeats in the palm of his hand.

It took an eternity for the elevator to come back up to the thirty-third floor. When it opened, Trev dropped to his knees.

Claire was standing there—still wrapped in her pathetic towel.

"He let me go," Claire said, her voice breathy. Her eyes darted from Trev to Sam. "Why did he let me go?"

Sam stepped into the elevator and wrapped her arms around Claire. She was nearly an entire head taller than the blonde girl.

"What do we do now?" Claire's voice was muffled—she was still enveloped in Sam's arms.

"We find him," Sam said to the top of Claire's head. "But first we find you some clothes."

Chapter 6

Dom saw lights on at his house when Julia pulled into his driveway. "Home sweet home, huh?" Collins said from the passenger seat, grinning back at Dom.

"Um, yeah," Dom mumbled. Why were there lights on? Had Trev come home? Dom pictured his phone tucked into one of Julia's pockets. How had people even functioned before cell phones? He hadn't heard from Trev in a few hours and it was ruining his life.

They walked Dom up to the front door, and then just let themselves in. Dom was preparing himself to yell—to warn Trev or Sam or whoever had returned to their house—but then he saw strangers walking around the living room and standing in the kitchen pointing up at the ceiling.

"Who the fuck are they?" Dom asked. He felt something—part livid, frothing anger and part fear—battle it out in the pit of his stomach.

"These are my people," Julia said. "They're going to help you."

Dom imagined for a moment that she meant *her people* as in a different species entirely, but he knew she meant Gregory's people. With a sinking stomach it dawned on him who they really were.

He had finally met the Wardens.

He had heard things from Trev and Sam—how the Wardens had driven their father crazy. How they wanted to take Trev and Sam in after their whole family was either dead or in jail, but the twins had run away. *What,* Dom had asked them over and over again, *was so horrible about the Wardens?* Besides, of course, the melodramatic name they had given themselves. He had never gotten a clear answer—at least not one that convinced him that turning your back on a whole society of ghost hunters (and all their history and knowledge) was a good thing.

"They're dead inside." That was what Trev had told him. But maybe Trev was wrong? Maybe they really could help?

He could hear Sam protesting in his head, *They broke into your house. They pointed a gun at you.* But the part of him that had been trying to hold it together for so long now—trying to figure out the whole world of ghosts with just Trev and Sam—wanted the Wardens to be an answer.

"So," Dom said, trying to sound calm—even cheerful. "Want to fill me in? If we're going to work together, maybe you should tell me what's going on."

There were five people in the house—not including Dom, Julia, and Collins. They looked to be in their late-twenties or early thirties except for one man who might have been in his fifties. They were all wearing very regular-looking clothes: jeans, button-up shirts, or T-shirts. They didn't look like some scary, mysterious secret society. Especially not one with millions of dollars to throw around.

Julia motioned for Dom to take a seat, as though it was her house and not his. Okay, so it wasn't really Dom's house (Trev and Sam had bought it) but the principle was the same. "Dominick, let me introduce you to everyone." She rattled off a list of names that Dom didn't even try to remember. He was too fucking tired for that.

In the kitchen light Julia looked younger again. Her dark hair did have long streaks of gray, and she did have lines around her mouth like she was accustomed to frowning, but she really didn't look that much older than him. She looked like a teenager who had been made up to look older. It was almost unnerving.

And her hand was worse than he had initially thought. She was actually missing two of her fingers. Luckily for her and her propensity to point guns at people, she still had her trigger finger.

"You keep talking about a war," Dom said. "What war? Obviously you mean ghosts, but I don't exactly see tanks driving down the street or ghost soldiers. Come to think of it, I don't actually see that many ghosts."

"There is a war," Julia continued. "One that most of the population can't see or even comprehend. It has come down to a choice between the living and the dead. Both cannot exist on this earth anymore.

"That's what we have been trying to do, for years. It isn't enough to just simply destroy the ghosts that come through—we have to destroy the Doors themselves. If we don't do something, the dead are going to consume us."

Dom shook his head at Julia. "You keep talking about the ghosts like they're something else—some aliens or demons. But they're us. They used to be alive. We'll die and then we'll become ghosts, too."

The other Wardens were listening to their conversation. A few of them were frowning at Dom.

"There is a realm for the dead," Julia continued, "and it isn't here. They don't belong here with us. They had their turn, and now they need to be gone. The world wasn't meant to hover on the edge like this. The dead need to stay dead."

"How do you know the Doors aren't there for a reason?"

Julia narrowed her eyes at Dom. "You know so little about the things you have devoted your life to. Why is that?"

Dom wanted to say something like, *Why is your face is so stupid?*, but he had to remind himself that he wasn't talking to Sam. "I don't know," Dom answered, though he doubted that it was the type of question that actually warranted a response. "I think we've reached the point in the conversation where you should just say what you mean, instead of asking cryptic questions."

Julia smiled again, "Don't mind me. I'm just seeing what type of person our new recruit is."

Recruit? "And what type is that?" Dom asked.

"Brave, I think. Smart, if what Gregory told us is true. I think you'll fit right in."

"Why don't we call Gregory?" Dom wondered which one of Julia's pockets held his phone.

Julia shook her head. "No need. He knows we're here. He knows the plan."

"And the plan would be . . . ?"

"We'll tell you once Gregory gets back. He should be here soon."

Chapter 7

The ferry was almost empty when they drove on, so they were waved up to the front. Trev figured that there weren't many commuters at one-something in the morning. Sam had been silent during the walk to the car and then the short drive to the ferry. Trev had tried to talk to her about a plan, but she had just waved him off.

After they were parked, Sam got out of the car and headed for the passenger area. She didn't wait to see if Trev or Claire wanted to come, and soon she was gone from sight.

Claire was sitting in the backseat with Jackson. His head was propped up on her shoulder, and one arm draped dangerously close to her chest. Had Jackson not been Jackson (and had he been conscious), it would have almost looked like he was trying to feel Claire's boobs. "Go after her," Claire said to Trev, nodding toward the direction that Sam had headed. "She shouldn't be alone."

"She's fine," Trev said, wincing at how sharp his voice sounded. The last thing he wanted was to get out of the car and walk up a flight of stairs.

"No," Claire said, her tone impatient. She rolled her eyes, but didn't otherwise move—afraid of disturbing Jackson. "Sam isn't fine. She is a fucking mess. And what if Gregory is on this ferry? Do you really want her to be alone?"

Trev nodded toward Jackson. "Can you keep an eye on him?" With the dome light on Trev could see that blood had dripped down Jackson's arm and was staining the carpet. *Sorry, Dom* . . . not that his car was in perfect shape to begin with.

"We'll be fine," Claire said. "And if we aren't,

I'll call you, okay? So don't drop your phone over the side."

Trev tried to smile, though his face didn't completely cooperate. He felt like he was wearing a rubber mask. "I'll do my best."

Trev found his sister staring at the vending machine. At first he thought Sam was trying to decide what to buy, but then he noticed that she wasn't looking at the chips or candy bars. Sam was staring at her own reflection.

"Hey," Trev said, sidling up to her until their shoulders touched. He thought she might move away from him, but she leaned toward him until Trev felt like he might just be the only thing holding her up. "How are you feeling?"

Sam gave an ugly, snorting laugh. "Oh, I'm feeling just peachy, and yourself?"

"I feel like I could run a marathon. Or maybe

a triathlon. Actually, do you run triathlons? Or is that swimming?"

Sam shrugged, then cocked her head like she was remembering something. "Actually," she said, "I think it's both. And maybe biking, too, right?"

"Well, shit, let's go sign up. They say you never forget how to ride a bike."

"You never forget a lot of things," Sam said softly, and Trev knew that she hadn't forgiven him for the way things went down with Jackson. That maybe she never would. Well, he still hadn't forgiven her for punching him in the face and running away to Seattle. That wasn't true. He had forgiven her the moment she opened the hotel door, the instant he saw her face and knew she was alive.

Trev pulled out his wallet. He opened it and saw that he still had his room keycard. He wondered how much the damage would cost in Sam's room, and what the hotel would think of all the blood. They hadn't even tried to clean it up.

He tossed the card toward a nearby garbage, and it bounced off the rim. Neither of them moved to pick it up.

"What do you want?" Trev asked, motioning toward the vending machine with his wallet. "My treat."

"What do you think happened when Jackson died?" Sam asked, completely ignoring his question. "It was so close, Trev. I didn't think I could bring him back. I shouldn't have been able to do it. He should be dead now."

Trev had no idea how to answer, so he fed a few dollars into the machine and punched buttons at random. A stick of gum fell down. *Damn.* He fed in a few more dollars.

"Do you think Dad . . . " Sam continued. "Do you think the ghost is still inside him? The one that made him do it?" They had never gone to visit their father in prison. Trev had never wanted to see him, but he wondered what kind of man they would find. And, buried deep in the back of his brain, Trev wondered if they had abandoned their father—if they had given up on him.

"I don't know," Trev finally said. He punched a few more buttons, and this time a Kit Kat bar fell out. He reached down and picked it up. After removing the wrapper, Trev broke the candy bar in half and handed Sam one of the sections, just like they were in a fucking commercial. She took her half and then turned and walked away.

He watched her open the door and go out onto the deck. Chocolate melted on his fingers as he watched the door close behind her. It would be so easy to just go back down to the car and not have to deal with Sam and her moody shit anymore.

Sighing, he followed her outside.

She was leaning against the railing. Her arms, he realized with a twist of guilt, were bare. Sam must have left her coat in the car. Trev almost took off his own coat and draped it over her shoulders but he knew she'd never accept it. For all he knew she might even shrug it off over the side of the boat into the dark water beneath.

He stood beside her, pressed against the cold of the metal railing, until finally the silence became a living thing between them. Something with scales and fangs. "Do you know why I broke up with Gregory?" Trev finally said.

She turned to him and shook her head. "You never told me." There was hurt in her voice.

Trev looked down into the darkness, wondering how many dead things were hidden beneath the waves. "He told me that he was working with the Wardens—the people who did that to Dad. They're not bad, he said. They're trying to save the world. That's what they think at least. That's what Gregory thought."

When she didn't say anything, Trev continued, "I don't know what Gregory's done to himself, but did you see his eyes? Could you feel what was inside him? Those were ghosts. They're using ghosts, Sam. They're not destroying them—

they're harnessing them somehow. It doesn't seem right. It seems . . . " Trev tried to find a word for the *wrongness* he had felt when he looked at Gregory. "It's like what happened to Jackson, only they're inviting the ghosts inside them. They opened the fucking door to their heads and said come on in."

Trev had been looking down at the water, not wanting to see his sister's face when she realized what he had kept from her all those months. Finally, when she still didn't speak, he turned to her. She was watching him, her eyes filled with tears. Sam wasn't really crying—not making any sounds or scrunching up her face like she used to do when they were younger and she would sob loudly and dramatically. Her face was calm, but tears welled up in her eyes and overflowed.

She took a deep breath, then whispered, "Why didn't you tell me?"

Trev shook his head. "You didn't need to know."

"Oh Trev, what do you mean I didn't need to know? Of course, I did. Did you think I couldn't handle it? Did you think I would freak out? That I would do something stupid? That's what you always think: *Sam's gonna go do something reckless and stupid. Sam's gonna need to be rescued again.*"

"No." Trev looked at the water again. He couldn't bear to see those silent tears slide down his sister's face.

"Then what? I deserved to know. I deserved to know exactly why we left Texas, and why you hated Gregory. Do you think I would have called him if I knew that he was with *those* people? Texted him? Do you think I would have given him our fucking address?" She paused and rapped her knuckles along the railing. It gave off a dull, metal sound.

Why hadn't he told her? Why had it been so important to keep it locked away in a secret room in his heart where he could hate Gregory in private? "Sam, I . . . " Trev sighed, leaning his head further over the railing. The smell of the Puget Sound prickled his nose and made him think of schools of fish and whales and other things hidden from sight. "I just," he finally said, looking up at her again. "I didn't want you to hate him too. I thought I could do it for the both of us."

She stared at him. "You're still in love with him, aren't you?"

"Don't be stupid."

"You are," she said. He didn't know if she meant he was still in love with Gregory, or that he was stupid. Or both. He didn't ask, and she didn't say anything else. She just put her cold arm around his shoulder and pulled him to her.

They spent the rest of the ferry ride watching the Seattle lights grow dimmer and finally fade over the horizon. Sam's bare arms shone in the dark like pale flames.

As Trev drove off the ferry, Sam tried to call Dom again, but there was still no answer.

"Maybe he's just asleep?" Claire volunteered in her fake cheerful voice. "Maybe he left his phone in the other room or the ringer got turned off? I've done that before."

Trev seriously doubted that Claire had ever been without her phone for longer than five seconds at a time. She probably slept with her phone.

He glanced in the rearview mirror. Jackson wasn't asleep anymore. He was watching Trev. Their eyes met in the mirror, and Jackson looked away.

In that instant, Trev was back in the kitchen in the yellow house, watching Gregory walk toward Jackson with the belt. Trev was going to let Gregory do it—he was going to watch while Gregory murdered Jackson. And somewhere, buried deep inside his own body by Eli's ghost, the real Jackson had been watching.

Trev turned his eyes back to the empty road in front of him.

There was still more than an hour's drive until they reached Grey Hills. Trev didn't want to think about what they might find.

Chapter 8

When Gregory got to the yellow house around two in the morning, he came in and sat down at the kitchen table just like he belonged there—like it was his house.

"Where's Trev?" Dom asked when his friend didn't immediately follow Gregory through the front door.

Julia and some of the other Wardens turned to Gregory, too—apparently they weren't quite in the loop either.

"Trev's in Seattle," Gregory said. "He's still looking for Sam and Jackson."

There was something about Gregory's voice—

maybe it was how calm he sounded, or even just the way he said Trev's name—that made Dom's chest tighten. Gregory had such a cavalier tone, as though it didn't matter to him one way or another if Trev was alone in a strange city.

"You just left him?" Dom asked. "Why?"

"My people needed me here," Gregory said, smiling across the table.

Dom glanced at Julia. She was frowning at Gregory—but she seemed to frown at everyone, so maybe she didn't think anything was strange. "Hey," Dom said to her. "Can I get my phone back now? I want to see how Trev's doing."

She started to say something, but Gregory interrupted her. "I don't think that's a good idea, Dominick," he said, nodding toward the other Wardens who were gathering around them. "You know how Trev feels about us."

"This is bullshit!" Dom stood up, looking at all the strange faces around him. "This is my fucking house. And those are my friends. You can't stop me from calling them."

"Your house . . . " Gregory ducked his head, then shook his hair out of his eyes. He needed a goddamn haircut. "You know, Dominick, it is really late. I think Trev is probably asleep by now anyway. Just call him tomorrow at a reasonable hour. There is no point in waking him up just to tell him that you don't actually have any news."

"Um, I have lots of news." Dom was going to start listing everything he might potentially tell Trev: that strangers with guns were in their house; that Gregory was acting like a total asshole; the gun thing, again. That was worth mentioning at least twice.

Gregory, however, started talking again before Dom could continue. "Helpful news?" Gregory asked. "Anything he can use to find Sam? Anything that will help him save Jackson?" Gregory smiled again.

Dom never remembered him smiling like that

before—as if Dom was a child and he was humoring him. Was this the real Gregory? Had the Gregory he'd known in Texas just been pretending to be a decent guy? Had he just pretended to be their friend?

Besides the aforementioned grievances, Dom did have something to tell Trev—he just didn't want Julia and the others to know. He thought he knew where to find the journal. "Look, just tell me," Dom said. "Am I a prisoner here?"

Gregory didn't answer right away. He held Dom's gaze, watching him with that new, condescending smile.

Then he said, "Of course not. But you have to understand that this is a very sensitive time right now. We have to make smart moves. And having you call Trev and freak him out so he comes running home without finding his sister—that is not smart."

Dom stared at him in disbelief.

"Dominick," Gregory continued. "Why don't you get some rest? You must be exhausted."

Dom lay in Sam's bed. He'd been using her room since she left because his room had that freaky crack in it. He didn't really know what sleeping next to a possible gateway to the dead might do to a person. It would probably cause more than bad dreams.

He could hear the Wardens talking down the hall, but he couldn't quite hear what they were saying. Dom felt like he was a child and had been sent to his room with no dinner. Actually, he *hadn't* eaten dinner, but he wasn't especially hungry.

Dom pulled out the Altoids tin and shook it, listening to the few remaining pain pills rattle around. That was the sound time made when you pressed it down into a little pill and kept it in a box.

That was how many hours he had left before the pain came back and grabbed his shoulder with its sharp pincer fingers.

Dom opened the tin and tipped one of the pills into his mouth. He bit down, cracking the bitter pill apart with his teeth, then waited for the pain to ease. The pain came and went like the swells that pass beneath a boat when you are already too far out to sea for the wave to break. It lifted him, and then he sank back down into a cool, watery hollow.

He closed his eyes, willing his mind to shut down long enough for him to sleep. If he couldn't do anything about the people in his house tonight, he could at least go somewhere else for a few hours. Maybe he would dream.

Then he remembered Sam's phone.

Dom almost cried out in relief. How had he forgotten? The phone was in the drawer of Sam's bedside table. Dom had put it there himself after Trev left, and Dom got sick of looking at Sam's pictures. When he looked at the pictures from the Halloween party—the ones with a glimpse of Macy's red cape—Dom couldn't stop running that night through his head over and over again.

When Macy kissed him that night, something inside him had changed. Maybe his heart, if he could stand the cliché. It was like the Grinch in that Christmas movie—Dom's heart grew three sizes, and he had given it to her. And now it wouldn't fit back in his fucking chest.

He had buried it in her grave.

Each time he looked at the pictures, a sharp, longing pain in his chest told him that, if he really tried, he could reach through the screen and go back to that night. That he could keep Macy from leaving the house. That he could keep her alive.

Dom held his breath while he opened the drawer, as though Julia could hear him—or maybe even hear his thoughts. As he fumbled in the dark drawer for Sam's phone, his hand brushed across a small plastic baggie. Dom recoiled, and then made himself pick it up. He held the baggie out in front of him, then shoved it into his pocket. It was Macy's Token.

After Sam left, Dom had tried to finish the Token. He had wound Macy's hair around the finger-bone, then wrapped a cloth around it and tied the whole thing with a red ribbon he'd cut from her cloak. But it didn't work. Macy hadn't come back.

Dom reached in the drawer again and found the phone. He pressed the button to turn on the screen, but nothing happened.

The battery was dead.

Sam's charger was still plugged in next to the table. Dom had to try three times to plug the end of the charger into the phone. He kept doing it upside down, or he thought it was upside down.

He dropped it once, and then froze, listening for footsteps. Nothing.

When he finally had it plugged in the screen lit up, and the little battery symbol blinked. Dom typed in the password (he had changed it from *duck shit* to *my car bitch*) and then pulled up Trev's name.

Sam answered on the second ring. "Dom? That's my phone."

"Sam?" Dom pulled the phone away from his face and double checked the number. It was definitely Trev's. Then it all hit him. Whispering so Julia and others wouldn't hear, he said, "Trev found you? Are you both okay? Is Jackson . . . ?"

"Oh my God, Dom. Where are you? Are you at home? Why haven't you been answering your fucking phone?" Then Sam was talking so fast the Dom could barely understand her. He had to lean over the little table because the phone charger would only stretch so far. Dom tried to sit up, but the charger pulled out of the phone and the line went dead.

"Shit!" he hissed under his breath, scrambling to plug it back in. As soon as the charger was back in place the phone was ringing in his hand. Dom picked up, hoping no one heard the one short ring. "Sam?" he whispered. "I'm back."

"Where are you?"

"I'm at home, but there are a bunch of people here. The Wardens. They have guns—one gun at least. And Gregory's here too but he's working with the Wardens. He's being a real dick and wouldn't let me call you, but I found your phone and—"

"Gregory's there? Get out of the house right now. Just go. Start running."

"The phone needs to charge," Dom said, feeling slow and stupid—surely there was something more important to say.

"What?" Sam said, an exasperated edge to her

voice. "It doesn't matter. Just get outside. We're almost there. We'll find you."

Dom heard something down the hall—maybe in the kitchen. A loud crash. He got off the bed and walked toward the door, stretching the cord as far as it would go. It must have completely sucked to use those old landlines with cords—Dom felt like a dog on a leash. Another crash and someone yelling.

"Dom?" Sam said on the phone, "Did you hear me? Get the fuck out now."

"Just a sec, I have to tell you something."

"It can wait."

Dom shook his head, though Sam, of course, couldn't see it. "No. That's what always happens in movies. People always wait to say the really important stuff, and then one of them dies."

"Jesus Christ. This isn't a movie. And you are going to die now if you don't get out of that house. Eli is inside Gregory." Sam's voice choked up, and Dom wasn't sure if he'd heard that last part right.

"What?"

"Eli Grey, the scary fucking ghost, is inside Gregory. Now get out of there."

Eli was inside Gregory? What happened to Jackson? Dom had missed everything. He felt as though someone had changed the channel on him, and he was watching an entirely different show. And they still didn't have Eli's Token to control him.

"The journal!" Dom exclaimed, momentarily forgetting to be quiet. "Eli's journal, the Token, it wasn't in the grave. I think it's in the Opal—that old movie theater. The ghost in the theater—her name was Mabel. I think Eli hid the journal with Mabel's ghost."

There was either stunned silence on the other end, or the call had dropped. He looked at the screen, and it was still connected. "Sam? Still there?"

"Yeah? That's great! If we can just get that journal . . . Yeah, Trev, I told him about Eli . . . okay, now Dom, get out of that house. Just go. You don't know . . . you haven't seen what Eli can really do. Just run." The call ended.

Dom ripped the charger out of the wall and stuffed it and the phone into his pocket. Then he ran.

Chapter 9

The screaming began right when Dom started to open Sam's bedroom door. He snatched his hand away from the doorknob, as though his touch had caused the screaming. Then he shook his head and opened the door.

Dom ran out into the hall. He had to go past the kitchen to get to the front door. When Dom got to the kitchen he stopped and clutched his hand to his mouth. The kitchen smelled like burnt hair and blood.

There was so much blood.

At least three of the Wardens were dead, though Dom couldn't tell right away what exactly had killed them. The bodies and the blood all blurred together. It looked like one of them had his throat ripped out. Another was missing an arm.

Dom made himself keep moving.

He was almost to the front door when he heard it. A woman screaming, coming from upstairs.

Don't, Dom told himself. *You can't help her.* He closed his eyes and saw the flash of Macy's red cape, the way it was in the picture on Sam's phone. Just out of reach, then gone.

Dom turned to run toward the stairs, then stopped. He went back to the kitchen, stepped over one of the dead bodies, and opened a drawer by the sink. There it was, just like Sam had said: the master key to all the locks in the house— right by the manual to the microwave.

Stupid-stupid-stupid pounded his heart. *Get the fuck out*, said Sam's voice in the back of his head. Dom remembered when Jackson (Eli, actually) had lifted his glowing arms and flung Dom against the wall. The air had crackled around Dom as Jackson's power washed over him. It had reminded him of how it had felt when the Door to the Dead opened behind the school. The pressure and the electric crackling . . . the sensation that time had slowed.

As he ran up the stairs, Dom felt it again. The hair on his arms and the back of his neck stood up, and the air crackled. He smelled something metallic, and his tongue felt fuzzy. When he touched the doorknob to his old bedroom, a blue spark jumped, shocking him.

Dom tried to turn the handle, and sure enough, it was locked—though why, Dom suddenly wondered, had Eli bothered to lock it? With a shaking hand he put the key in the doorknob and turned. The door opened.

Inside he found Gregory holding a woman by the neck, her face pressed to the light in the floor. Collins' body was next to the bed. His face was blackened and cracked, as though someone had held a blowtorch to his skin.

Dom could only tell it was Collins from the leather jacket and the size of him. When Dom heard the woman screaming, he had thought it would be Julia, but it was another Warden whose name he couldn't remember. He hadn't even bothered to try to learn their names, and now they were dead.

He thought he was going to throw up.

Stop! That is what Dom wanted to yell, but he couldn't make himself speak. The air smelled like burned flesh and something sharper, more metallic—all Dom could think was *electric blood.*

Gregory looked up and saw Dom. He smiled. Gregory may have said something, but Dom couldn't hear any words over the sound of the woman screaming.

Then Dom heard a voice that he shouldn't have been able to hear. It sounded as close as a whisper in his ear and as loud a megaphone in his mind.

Close your eyes. It sounded like Macy.

He closed his eyes, and then the world exploded.

Chapter 10

After Trev dropped Claire off at her house, she quietly unlocked the front door and went inside. They had taken Jackson to a hospital on their way to Grey Hills. It was dangerous to leave him somewhere so public, even though they had given the staff a fake name. The police were still looking for Jackson, and, of course, they'd be checking hospitals. But it was either that or watch Jackson die (again) from whatever injuries he had sustained over the past few days.

Apparently it was the same hospital where Trev and Sam had taken Dominick after he was shot the night of the Lock-In. Claire had learned about that *minor* detail on the long drive home.

Every now and then Claire just wanted to punch Macy in the arm for keeping so many secrets from her. They had only been best friends since the seventh fucking grade.

But no, Macy just *had* to hide this huge part of her life from Claire. She wished she could ask Macy *why*? Why couldn't Macy just trust that Claire would believe her? That Claire would help her? But when you ask the dead questions, they don't usually answer.

Unless . . .

Claire couldn't stop thinking that if she just tried hard enough she could be able to see Macy's ghost. With so many people around her who could see ghosts, it felt like a character flaw that she couldn't. Was her brain just too lazy? Was she too stupid? Was that why Macy didn't tell her? Did Macy think that Claire was too much of a useless idiot to help them?

Claire took off her shoes and slowly walked up the stairs. She had a story ready in case her mom woke up. When Claire followed Sam to Seattle, she had called her mom and told her that she needed to get out of Grey Hills for a few days—it was just too painful to be here after they'd found Macy's body. If her mom found her creeping up the stairs at three in the morning, Claire planned to start crying and tell her mom that she woke up at her dad's house, and she just *needed* her mom. Then they'd hug, Claire would cry into her shoulder, and that would be that.

The funny thing was that it wasn't really a lie. Well, the "dad's house" part was a complete lie, but Claire kind of hoped that her mom would come out and ask her what the hell she was doing driving home in the middle of the night. She wanted her mom to pull her close and run her fingers through her hair and tell her that everything would be okay.

Claire wanted to believe that things *could* be okay, even for a moment.

She crept past her sister's room on the way to her own, and then stopped. Claire reached out and placed her hand on her sister's doorknob. Slowly, she opened the door.

Sabrina's room smelled like vanilla body spray. Claire had originally bought it for herself, but got sick of it and gave her sister the half-empty bottle. The room smelled like Beenie had poured it all over her bed and clothes.

After stepping lightly across the messy floor, Claire crawled into her sister's bed. Beenie groaned and turned over. "Claire?" she murmured in a groggy voice. "Am I dreaming?"

"Yeah," Claire whispered, brushing her sister's hair out of her face. "Go back to sleep."

Beenie gave her a look that was equal parts skeptical and sleepy and then turned over and snuggled back into her pillow.

Claire draped her arm around her sister's waist and pulled her close.

"Claire?" Beenie whispered.

"Yeah?" Claire's head barely fit on the pillow, and it smelled sickeningly like vanilla. She wished she could stop time, and just stay here forever.

"Macy's dead, isn't she?" asked Sabrina's tiny, hesitant voice. Of course her sister would have heard about Macy's body by now. Claire tried to imagine their mother sitting Sabrina down and telling her what happened. She should have been with her sister for that.

Tears began to stream down Claire's face and soak into the pillowcase. She didn't wipe them away, because she didn't want to let Beenie go.

"Yeah," Claire whispered.

Beenie didn't talk for a little while, and Claire started to hope that she had just gone back to sleep, but then her sister said, "I saw her."

"What?" Claire nearly choked on her own breath. "What do you mean you saw her?"

"I don't know. It's stupid."

"No. Tell me. What do you mean you saw her?" Claire sat up. Sabrina sat up, too, so she was facing Claire.

"I thought I saw Macy in the hall, a few days after she went missing. Just for a second. She was standing outside your door, but then she was gone. She vanished." Her sister's voice was shaking. It was too dark to see Sabrina's face, but Claire knew there would be a little crease right between her eyebrows, which meant she was trying not to cry.

Claire pressed her lips together until she knew that her own tears weren't going to completely melt her face. Then she said, "But that's impossible."

"That's why I didn't tell you. I thought . . . I thought I had seen her ghost. I thought it meant that she was dead. And now she is. Mom said that . . . "

Claire frowned. How much did Sabrina know

about the way Macy died? Claire wasn't even sure if the police would have released any details yet. Could their mom have possibly told Beenie that Macy's throat had been cut? Jesus . . . she hoped not.

"Do you think it was real?" her sister asked softly. "Do you think Macy's ghost was really here?"

Claire could feel the truth like a hard, sour candy on her tongue. "No," Claire said. "I'm sure it was a dream." The words were easier to say than she expected. Lies always were.

Beenie nodded. Even in the shadows, Claire could see the way she tucked her chin down toward her chest. "Yeah . . . I knew it wasn't real. Sorry."

Claire pulled her sister into a hug. "Don't ever apologize to me, okay?"

They lay back down in the bed, and Claire kept her arm around her sister. She could feel

Beenie's breath and heard when it changed to the deep rhythm of sleep.

Claire closed her eyes. She was so tired. She knew she should go to her own room and her own bed where she wouldn't have to share a pillow with her preteen sister, but the thought of moving again made her limbs ache.

Just a few minutes, Claire told herself. *Just a few more minutes.*

Claire woke knowing she was in pain, but not knowing why. And it wasn't necessarily pain. It was more of an uncomfortable pressure—the feeling that she had been plunged deep underwater, and her body wasn't given time to adjust. Her ears were too full—almost painfully so—and her teeth throbbed.

Beenie was whimpering in her sleep. Claire pulled her arm out from under her sister's head and sat up. Her heart was racing—pounding as if it were trying to escape from her ribcage. She ran her hand through her hair, and the strands crackled with static electricity.

Her mouth tasted like blood.

What the fuck? Claire remembered taking her phone out of her pocket when she first got into her sister's bed because a corner had been jabbing her in the leg. She got down on her hands and knees and felt for the plastic rectangle on the ground. After a few really long seconds, her fingers grazed the smooth screen.

She turned the screen on. The light from her phone was so bright that Claire had to look away for a moment so her eyes could adjust. She'd only been asleep for about fifteen minutes.

No wonder she still felt like she'd been run over by several cars, and then maybe kicked by a horse or two. She was exhausted.

Claire got up and went to the door. She was about to go to her own room when another wave of that strange pressure-pain swept over her. It was though all of the air had been squeezed out of her lungs. She dropped to her knees, her hand still on the doorknob.

What was happening to her?

Chapter 11

"Just run!" Sam yelled at Dom over the phone, and then hung up so he would do what she fucking said and get of there. Gregory was in their house? With Dom? *Fuck, fuck, fuck!*

She took a deep breath and focused on how slowly the trees and houses were moving past them. "Drive faster!" Sam snapped at her brother. "You drive like a ninety-year-old woman."

Trev didn't say anything—sarcastic or otherwise. He put his foot down, and the world whipped past a little faster.

Finally they turned onto their familiar street. Sam recognized the bump of a particular root-cracked bit of pavement, and then she saw an old playground in someone's yard that meant they were only two blocks away from the yellow house.

"We'll pick up Dom," Sam said. "Then we'll go to the movie theater. We'll get the journal and come back." She looked at her brother. "Trev, we'll come back for Gregory. I'm not giving up."

Trev nodded. His hands were gripping the steering wheel, and his mouth was turned down at the corners. Sam put her own hand on the car door—ready to let Dom in so they could drive off again, quickly.

Then they were pulling up to the yellow house. The lights were on, but Sam didn't see anyone moving in the windows.

She didn't see Dom.

"Goddamn it!" She slammed the heel of her hand on the car door. "Where the hell is he?"

"He'll be here," Trev said. His voice sounded like something scraped off the bottom of a boat. "He's going to open the door any second."

While they sat in the idling car watching the front door, Sam's mouth started to taste funny. Her tongue was tingling, like when the Novocain wore off after getting a cavity filled.

Then her hair began to float around her head. A piece drifted into her mouth, and she spat it out. "Trev?" she whispered, reaching over to grab his arm. "Do you feel that?"

He nodded, then ran a hand over his own hair. "What's happening?"

"I don't know." Sam opened the car door. "Where is he? I think I should go in there."

It was Trev's turn to grab Sam's arm. "Stop," he said, "do you hear that?" They listened. Sam thought she heard screaming.

"That's it, I'm going in." As she swung her legs out of the car a light exploded in front of her. She was thrown back into the car, and she felt the whole frame of the car sway from the impact of whatever had just happened. Sam's back hit the stick shift, and her head was knocked into Trev's chest.

Sam tried to sit up, but Trev's arms were wrapped around her. "Close the car door!" She heard her brother yell. She tucked her legs back inside the car and, struggling out of his grasp, sat up and slammed the car door shut. She locked it for good measure.

"What just happened?" she yelled. It was hard to even hear her own voice. Her ears were ringing.

Trev was saying something else—she could hear his voice in the background like a distant river—but by then all she could focus on was the sight before her. The house was glowing with a blue light.

It looked exactly like the Door to the Dead behind the school when it had first opened: bright and terrible and pulsing as though to a rhythm Sam couldn't hear. Only this was bigger. This was as big as the fucking house.

"Go," Sam whispered. She couldn't feel her lips move. The pressure in her chest was getting tighter and tighter. Trev's hand was on her shoulder, but she couldn't hear him. All she could see was the blue light rippling and growing. Oh God, it was growing!

"Go!" She repeated, louder this time. Then she was screaming, "Drive, Trev! Just drive!" because something was coming out of the blue light. Not some*thing* but *things*. Ghosts, she quickly realized. Dozens of ghosts. They spilled out of the house like hornets from a big fucking nest.

And then the light was growing smaller again. It took Sam a moment to realize it was because Trev was doing exactly what she had said: he was driving, and fast.

Chapter 12

Claire was sitting on her sister's floor, holding Beenie in her lap while the young girl sobbed. There were ghosts in her room. Claire couldn't see them, but her sister could.

"Beenie?" Claire whispered into her sister's hair. "You know when you said you thought you saw Macy? And I told you it was a dream? I lied. I'm sorry."

Sabrina didn't say anything, but made a little whimpering sound. Moments earlier she had leapt into Claire's arms, saying there were people in the room. Beyond that, Claire hadn't gotten many details.

Claire got out her phone and called Sam. "What just happened?" Claire demanded as soon as Sam answered Trev's phone. "First, I felt like my head was going to explode, and now my house is apparently full of ghosts."

"You can see them?" Sam asked. Her voice sounded far away. Sam had put her on speaker phone, hadn't she? Annoying.

"No, I can't see them. My eleven-year-old sister can see them. Why can my eleven-year-old sister see fucking ghosts?" Claire mentally apologized to her sister for swearing.

"Claire, something bad happened."

"No fucking shit something bad happened. Are you guys okay?" Claire stroked her sister's head. It was really unnerving to know that there were probably ghosts right next to her face but she couldn't see them. What if one of the ghosts was like Eli? What if it jumped inside her or her sister? "Sam, what should I do? Are these ghosts going to, like, possess me? Or eat me? Should I run? I know you're not supposed to run from some animals because then they'll chase you, like bears, but I think you're *supposed* to run from other kinds of bears so I just don't know."

"Claire?" Sam said gently, "Get a fucking grip, okay? You're going to be fine. Most ghosts are harmless."

"Ghosts are harmless? Didn't we all just almost get killed by a ghost? And what happened anyway? Where did these ghosts come from?"

Sam paused, and then said, "Eli ripped open a Door to the Dead. We think that's what happened at least. And . . . we don't know where Dom is. I think he was in the house when the Door opened. It was like a bomb, Claire. And then all these ghosts came flooding out . . . "

"And now the ghosts are here, in my house?" In her lap, she could feel Sabrina's attention shift. She was listening. "It's going to be fine," she whispered to her sister, holding Sabrina closer with her free hand.

"How many ghosts does your sister see?"

"I don't know," Claire said, squinting into the dark room.

"Ask her."

Claire squeezed her sister, "Beenie, I need you to open your eyes again. How many ghosts, I mean, how many people do you see? How many people are in the room?"

"I don't know," Beenie said in a small voice thick with tears.

"Can you count them?" Claire asked, trying to sound encouraging, as though it was perfectly normal for her sister to be counting ghosts in the middle of the night. Just like counting sheep . . .

"I just see one."

"One? You only see one?" Claire let out a deep breath. When had *one* morphed into *my room is full of ghosts* in her sister's brain? She was probably failing math.

Claire repeated the number into the phone.

"Okay, that's fine," Sam said. "One is fine.

Just . . . slowly leave the house. Actually, don't leave the house. Go to another room. Just be quiet, and don't make too many big movements. Most ghosts won't even notice you're there."

"Can't you just come over and, you know, do whatever it is that you do to ghosts? Make it disappear?"

"We can't, Claire. We have to find the journal and stop Eli. And seriously, the ghost is probably harmless. Just move to another room and leave it alone. But . . . don't go outside, okay? I don't know how many are out there. Look, I have to go, but call me back if anything changes." Then Sam hung up.

Claire looked at the phone in disbelief. Sam actually hung up on her? Bitch! Claire was about to call Sam back and explain that yes, she and Trev *would* come over and take care of this ghost when Beenie spoke.

"Claire? I think we know him."

"What did you say?" Claire leaned down so her ear was closer to her sister's mouth.

Beenie's voice was almost too soft to hear when she said, "He looks like Macy's brother."

Chapter 13

When Sam and Trev broke into the Opal, it was well past three in the morning. Since most theaters didn't have showings much later than midnight (and this was a tiny, one-screen movie theater in a tiny, one-theater town), Sam wasn't worried that they were going to interrupt someone's movie-going experience.

Did it really count as a break-in if you didn't actually break anything? Sam wondered about that distinction as she pulled her lock-picking tools from a coat pocket and went to work. The metal pick flashed as she moved it deftly into the lock.

The nearest streetlight was at the end of the block, so it was nice and dark near the Opal's big front door. Sam saw a few ghosts wandering around the street, but they were just drifting aimlessly like plastic bags caught in the wind. She and Trev could deal with them and Claire's ghost later—after they found the journal.

Sam had been telling Claire the truth on the phone: most ghosts were harmless. It was just those few who might rip your throat out that you had to watch out for. Sam thought about the odds of Claire's little sister being able to see ghosts, and it was pretty miraculous. Was there something in the water in Grey Hills? Or maybe there really was just something special about the town itself.

It had produced Eli, hadn't it?

The shadows that concealed Sam were like a fabric pulled too tightly around her shoulders. It felt as though one wrong movement would burst a seam, and the darkness would unravel. If anyone spotted them—just one policeman driving past or one pedestrian out for a late-night stroll—they would lose their chance to find the journal.

On most days Sam and Trev were fairly innocuous looking: Trev possibly more so than Sam. Today, however, with their bloody clothes and wild hair, Sam was pretty sure a cop would think she and her brother were on drugs or had just committed a violent crime.

Or both.

Picking a lock was like riding a bike. That was what one of the YouTube videos she had watched had said. Sam didn't even understand what that was supposed to mean. Was it that you never forgot how to do it? Was it that you should wear a helmet? That you could fall off and skin your fucking knees?

Sam thought picking a lock was like trying to make scrambled eggs without breaking the shell.

Sliding her pick and a hairpin into the lock, Sam felt for the tumbler pins. This lock was old, maybe as old as the door itself, which could either be good or bad. Sometimes the pins started to stick and that made it tricky to get them all in the right position. Old locks, however, were often simple. She held her breath, listening for the first click of a pin sliding into place.

"Is it working?" whispered Trev.

"Quiet," hissed Sam. She closed her eyes, trying to picture the inside of the lock. When she was able to concentrate, her pick felt like an extension of her finger. The first pin clicked into place, but she met with resistance with the second. She slowly applied more pressure, imagining the pin lifting.

"How much longer is this going to take? I think I hear a car."

Sam ignored him. She pictured herself surrounded by a soundproof force field.

Click. Two pins were in place.

Her hand was starting to cramp up when she pushed the door open. "Tada," Sam whispered.

Trev said, "About fucking time."

"You're welcome," Sam said, letting Trev go in first. She shut the door behind them, wincing at how loud it sounded in the silence of the lobby.

"Where should we look first?" Sam asked. The only light in the room came from the window of the little ticket booth, so, for a moment, she didn't see what Trev was doing.

He had ducked behind the concessions counter and was already chewing on a candy bar.

"What the fuck, Trev? You're stealing?"

"I'm not stealing, I'm starving! Dinner was hours ago."

"Not cool."

"But breaking into a place is perfectly fine? Okay, I'll pay for it." Trev took out his wallet and pulled out a twenty. "Is this enough? I'm not completely familiar with the market rate of shitty chocolate."

Sam went over and snatched the money out of his hands. She crumpled the bill and stuffed it into her pocket. "Don't be stupid. You're not wearing gloves. What if they check for finger-prints?"

"Then I'll be known as an infamous candy bandit. Sounds good to me." Trev took another bite of the chocolate bar. "You owe me twenty bucks by the way. I'm adding it to my ledger."

"Whatever. Just finish your fucking chocolate. I think we should start with the actual theater—that's where Dom always saw the ghost, right?"

"Yeah," Trev replied. "Dom said that she just watched movies all day."

Dom.

Sam tried to push away the question that was beating both fists against her mind. *Is Dominick Vega alive?* When they drove away from the yellow house, Sam knew there was no other option. They had to go. Who knew if anyone inside the house had even survived the force of the Door ripping open. And there were so many ghosts . . .

Find the journal. That was all Sam could focus on now. Find that fucking journal. She could figure everything else out after Eli's Token was in her hands.

The door to the theater swung open silently. Sam had thought it would be perfectly dark in the empty room, but the emergency runner lights illuminated the ground at their feet. Sam didn't know if someone had forgotten to turn them off after the last movie, or if they were always lit.

"Hello?" Trev softly called to the empty rows of seats. "Mabel?"

Sam slowly walked down the aisle towards the screen, holding a flashlight out in front of her. She didn't really need it, but it made her feel better to have something in her hand.

There was a little stage at the front of the theater, presumably from when the Opal used to show plays instead of movies. She boosted herself up onto the stage, then closed the distance to the red curtain that covered the screen itself.

"Mabel?" Sam whispered, placing her hand on the curtain.

Before a movie, the curtains parted and rolled to the sides. Sam remembered that detail from the one time they had seen a movie here right after they arrived in Grey Hills. At the time, Sam had thought it was quaint and thought nothing more about it. Now, Sam wondered how old the curtain was. Old enough to have been splattered with Mabel's blood when she shot herself in the head? Probably not.

She pulled back one part of the curtain. The velvety fabric was almost greasy to the touch and it smelled like popcorn. She wondered if they ever washed the curtains.

Next Sam pressed her hands to the movie screen itself. She had thought it would feel different—maybe smooth but tough, like the canvas sail of a great boat. Instead, the screen felt textured, almost reptilian. There were thousands of tiny bumps on the surface.

"What do you think is back here?" Sam asked Trev, still trying to keep her voice low just in case someone could hear them from outside.

Trev was in the middle of one of the rows, checking each seat. "I don't know. Another, smaller theater for mice?"

Sam rolled her eyes. Trev was physically incapable of being serious. She pressed on the screen, and it billowed. "I think there is a space back here. I'm gonna check it out."

She took Macy's knife out of her pocket and flipped it open. Trev obviously saw what she was about to do and waved his hands in protest. "Jesus fuck, Sam. I can't take a one dollar candy bar and you can just destroy an entire movie theater? How are they going to show movies now? Total asshole move."

"I'll buy them a new screen, okay?" Sam hissed.

"Maybe I'll even pay for another fucking theater in this town, would that make you happy?"

She was about to plunge her knife into the screen when the back of her neck started to prickle. It felt like someone was holding a static-charged balloon behind her head.

Sam turned around, Macy's knife in one hand, and her flashlight in the other. Her mouth was almost too dry to swallow. "Hello?" Sam whispered.

"Did you see something?" Trev asked, loudly.

Sam waved her flashlight in his face. "Shhh!"

He swatted at the light and blinked, turning his face away, but he didn't say another word. That was probably a first for Trev.

Sam turned in a slow circle. When she looked toward the screen she had that feeling again: if she were to reach behind her, she thought she might touch someone.

Then a movie started to play.

Chapter 14

Sam leapt back, and the dark outline of her shadow stayed on the curtains in front of her. She watched in stunned silence as the curtains parted, rolling back to reveal all the colors of the movie in progress. There was no sound to the film, only the picture. A person was kneeling down, then someone was running.

Sam wanted to know what movie it was (had there been a NOW PLAYING poster outside the ticket booth?), but then she made herself come back to reality. And the reality was, there was someone in the projection room. Watching them.

"Trev!" Sam whispered, backing up to the edge of the stage. "Someone's up there."

A scene in the movie changed, and a car exploded. Sam almost fell off the stage. Then she and Trev jumped down, jogged up the aisle, and ran out of the theater.

They quickly found the door that led to the projection room. It was locked, but that was no problem for Sam. She had it open in three minutes. Not a personal best, but her hands were shaking.

Sam went first up the stairs, still holding the flashlight in her left hand and Macy's knife in the right. The stairway was narrow, and the stairs themselves seemed shallow and precarious—the kind you often find in old houses. Every third step or so Sam almost tripped, and then Trev would run into her back while she caught her balance.

At the top of the stairs was another door. This one was unlocked. Sam turned the handle slowly, then pushed it open, brandishing her knife.

The lights were on in the small room. It was cramped and full of what looked like really big computer towers. They made a humming sound and gave off a faint bluish light that reminded Sam of the light from the giant Door that had just consumed her house. But this light was purely mechanical—much like the blinking light any DVD player or laptop would emit. Sam suddenly felt like she was inside a robot's brain.

Besides the electronics, the room was empty.

"Do you see anything?" Trev asked.

Sam shook her head. Against the far wall was a desk with a computer monitor. The chair was pulled away from the desk and was moving ever so slightly, as though someone had just stood up and walked away.

"Hello?" Sam said softly. She didn't need the

flashlight anymore in the well-lit room, but she didn't want to put it down.

There was a small window that looked out into the theater. Sam stepped up to the glass and watched as the silent movie played on.

That's when she heard the chair move.

At first Sam thought it was Trev—that he had gravitated to the only chair in the room and sat down. But then she realized that Trev was still standing beside her, staring out the window.

Sam turned, and a woman was sitting in the chair. She was watching Sam, with a pensive expression on her face, as though she was trying to decide if Sam posed a threat. Which meant that this woman was smart, because Sam most certainly did.

The woman's head was a bloody mess.

"Mabel?" Sam asked, putting the knife back in her pocket. She didn't want to scare her away. Sam's heart was pounding, and she made herself breathe in and out slowly.

Trev, thank God, was silent.

The woman nodded her head like she had decided something about Sam and Trev. Maybe they had passed some kind of a test, because she started to speak.

"I like to come up here," the woman said. The ghost's voice had a lilt to it. It was almost child-like. "Sometimes I watch the films when no one else is here. I like it better when the movies are silent. There are too many words. Too many people talking. But I miss the music."

"Are you Mabel?" Sam asked. "Do you know Eli?"

The ghost had been looking past them to the window (and presumably to the movie beyond), but at the mention of Eli's name, her head turned sharply back toward Sam. Mabel touched the bleeding side of her head again. "I don't want to talk about Eli. Eli makes my head hurt."

"He's hurt a lot of people," Sam said slowly.

Mabel narrowed her eyes at Sam. "That is what he does."

"Do you have Eli's journal?" Trev blurted out from behind her.

Sam wanted to put her hand over her face. Thanks, bro. All the subtlety of a fucking hammer.

But Mabel actually nodded. "He told me to keep it safe. He made me. I have to do what he says."

"No, you don't." Sam took a step toward the ghost. She flinched, and Sam froze. "You don't have to do anything you don't want to do, Mabel. He can't hurt you anymore."

"He took a piece of me. He took it from my grave. Eli . . . or was it someone else? He didn't look like Eli then. He looked different."

Mabel touched her broken head and frowned. She flickered and then looked solid again. "He wanted to marry me," Mabel said in her soft, childlike voice. "He asked me before he died."

The ghost paused, and moved the chair in a lazy swivel. "I told him no.

"Then the Accident happened," Mabel continued. "That great explosion, and all those men died on the bluffs. Eli died, too. He was trying to stop it. I don't think there is anyone left who knows that part of the story. Someday I won't even remember. I've forgotten so many things. I thought I would forget him, too, one day. I hoped I would.

"Then Eli came back. He was inside my head. He said he would never leave me. I believed him, so I took my father's gun, and I came here. Eli tried to stop me, but he wasn't strong enough. At least, he wasn't strong enough back then. Maybe now he could have stopped me. I wasn't strong back then either. If I was stronger, maybe I could have lived with it—lived with him inside me.

"He said he loved me, right before I pulled the trigger. I thought, at the time, that it wasn't love. How can you crush the thing that you love? How can you smother it and hold it so close that it can't breathe?"

Mabel paused, and Sam wasn't sure if she was going to say anything more. The ghost's face grew fainter—less real somehow. Sam could see the computer monitor behind her head.

Then it looked as if Mabel took a deep breath and her face became solid once again. She kept talking.

"I used to think that love meant that you would die for someone. But now I think I was wrong. What if loving doesn't mean that you'd die for someone, but that you'd live for them? What if Eli really did love me? It has been one hundred years, and he always comes back. It's not life, but it's close. It's something."

Mabel smiled sadly. Sam could tell that she had been beautiful when she was alive. "Love hurts," the ghost whispered. "That's what all the writers say."

"Where is the journal?" Trev asked again. Sam could hear the rising panic in her brother's voice.

Mabel sighed. "You want to destroy him, don't you? I know that. I know a lot of things, now. Something changed—my mind was full of shadows and holes, but I remember so many things now." She held her hands out in front of her face. "I'm stronger now."

The ghost stood up and took a few steps toward Sam. "I did what Eli asked. I put his journal somewhere safe."

"But where is it?" Trev pleaded, and Sam shushed him.

"Mabel," Sam tried to catch the ghost's eyes, but Mabel was looking past her again—out to the movie that was still playing silently on the screen. "Please," Sam begged. "We can stop him. We won't let him hurt anyone else."

Mabel smiled that sad smile again. Her hand fluttered back up to the hole in her head. "I hid his journal with the one person who truly loved him." Then, just before she vanished, Mabel leaned closer, and whispered to Sam where she could find Eli's body.

Chapter 15

When Dom woke up he wasn't sure if he had really opened his eyes because it was still so dark. He was lying on his side on a hard, cold surface. Dom blinked against the blackness, then tried to move his hands up to his eyes. That was when he realized that his hands were tied behind his back.

Dom pulled at his bindings. They wouldn't give and dug into his wrists. It didn't feel like rope, but something smooth and sharp on the edges. Zip ties? He struggled until his shoulder ached from the effort. Dom tried to move his legs, but they were tied as well. Dom kicked and thrashed his legs, but nothing seemed to loosen them.

He did a quick mental calculation of his situation: he was hogtied in the dark and didn't have any idea where he was. *Wonderful.*

Then he remembered Gregory standing over the crack—feeding people to it. He remembered the dead Wardens in the kitchen, and how their blood was still wet. Most of all, he remembered the explosion. It had felt like the end of the world—as though every particle, every atom had burst apart.

The simplest explanation was that he was dead, and that God had a sick joke about the afterlife. But Dom didn't feel dead. Were dead people thirsty? Did dead people have an itch on their nose that they couldn't scratch because their hands were tied up? Negative on all accounts (he hoped).

What if Gregory had opened another Door to

the Dead and Dom was inside it? Was that possible? Was it cold and black through the Door?

Close your eyes. That was the last thing he remembered hearing. It had sounded like Macy . . .

Dom rolled onto his back and then sat up. He felt dizzy, and bright sparks flickered and swam before his eyes. He blinked again, swiveling his head from side to side. Once his eyes started to get a little more used to the darkness, he thought he could see the faintest difference when he looked to the right. Just a small brightening, like the solid black wasn't quite so thick in that direction.

The air was stale, but he could taste a tinge of brininess. He was somewhere near the water. But that wasn't very fucking helpful because the whole town of Grey Hills was near the water.

Even his own room in the yellow house had smelled like the ocean—especially in the morning when the fog curled around the bluffs and his window was so damp with dew that it seemed like the Puget Sound was trying to climb inside. He used to wake up from dreams that long arms of brown kelp were wrapped around his legs.

He wondered if his old room even existed anymore. Did the world exist?

Dom took a deep breath and then called out, "Hello?" His voice echoed back to him.

Wherever he was, it was an enclosed space.

He had heard of blind people who could actually use echolocation to *see* objects in a room. Dom gave a shrill whistle and tried to hear the shape of the room from the sounds that reverberated back. All he discovered was that he could not, in fact, magically learn echolocation in two seconds.

Reaching his bound hands toward the ground behind him, Dom felt a hard, smooth surface. Cement. Wherever he was (and he didn't really think it was through a Door) it seemed manmade. Was he in a garage? A basement? But it felt too cold to be in someone's house. And, he noticed, the cement felt slightly damp to the touch.

He had to get untied. Whatever was going to happen, it would be a million times better if he had the use of his hands. Dom put his legs out in front of him with his knees bent, then rocked himself forward until his momentum allowed him to stand. He wobbled, and those sparks in front of his eyes returned. Dom bent forward and breathed in a few deep, measured breaths until his head stopped spinning.

So he was standing . . . now what? Dom tried to remember movies where people were tied up. What did they do? They always seemed to find something sharp to cut through their bindings.

Dom took a tentative hop forward—he couldn't exactly walk with his legs tied at the ankles—and he felt a wave of vertigo. Another hop, and he hit a wall face first and fell back down to the ground.

One especially hot summer day when Dom was about eleven years old, his dad had taken him swimming. It was a local pool where Dom and his sister used to swim together. After Josie died, Dom had stopped wanting to go to the pool. His parents probably thought he was just grieving, but the real reason was because there was the ghost of a drowned boy who wanted to play with him in the shallow end of the pool.

Dom had ripped that boy apart just like he had his sister's ghost. It was so easy. Afterwards, Dom had started to cry—huge, racking sobs that never seemed to end. He started coughing and sucking up water. His mother had rushed over and scooped him out of the pool before he drowned and that was the end of the pool trips for several years.

When he was eleven years old, his parents were still trying to solve their son's "problems" on their own. They hadn't yet given up on trying to figure out what was wrong with their (now) only child's brain. That happened when he was fourteen, and they sent him across the country to a "special" school after he told a teacher that a dead classmate was trying to talk to him. A therapist said that Dom was acting out and had suggested that a different environment might help.

On that hot summer day when he was eleven, however, his dad decided they should go back to the pool. Their house was sweltering, and when they stepped outside, there was no breeze. Dom was covered in sweat by the time they reached the pool.

There were two ghosts in the changing room. Dom couldn't really tell what had killed them, so he assumed they had drowned. Dom didn't like the way they were watching him, so he quickly took care of them before he changed into his swimsuit. It was just too creepy to change in front of a ghost.

Dom wasn't sure if he would remember how to swim—it had been such a long time—but as soon as he was in the water, it came back to him. He started swimming from one end of the pool to the other, seeing how long he could stay under without coming up for air. Dom found he could swim to the far end of the pool without needing a breath. On the way back, however, he would start to get a frantic, tugging sensation deep in his chest, and he had to break the surface and suck in a lungful of air.

He kept trying and trying until he was exhausted, and then decided to try one final time. Dom made it to the far end, then turned around and swam back the other way. His lungs were burning, but he kicked extra hard, and, keeping his eyes closed, Dom reached out with his arms like he was flying. Just one more second, he kept telling himself. Just one more kick.

He was about to give up and go up for air, thinking that he wasn't even close, when his face slammed into the side of the pool.

Dom had opened his eyes and gasped from the

pain in his nose. The water clouded with what he didn't realize at the time was his own blood. Water filled his lungs, and Dom sank right to the bottom of the pool.

A lifeguard fished him out of the water and pounded on his back until Dom coughed up the bloody water he had inhaled.

Then his dad was standing above him, right where the lifeguard had been a moment before. Dom looked all around, but couldn't find the lifeguard anywhere. Across the pool was another lifeguard. She was reading a magazine and only looked up when Dom walked past her with the blood from his nose dripping into his cupped hand.

Dom's nose never healed quite right—it always looked slightly crooked. His dad never took him to the pool again. Dom went back several times on his own, looking for the lifeguard who had saved his life. He never found him, which was just

as well because Dom didn't know how to thank a
ghost for saving his life.

After Dom sat up again in the dark—wherever
it was that he was being kept—he wrinkled his
nose, trying to feel if any damage had been done
from slamming his head into a wall. Nothing
seemed to be broken, and he didn't think he was
bleeding.

When he stood up again, he leaned his back
against the wall and reached out with the tips of
his fingers. The wall felt like cement, too. Dom
found he could walk without actually hopping if
he took really small steps. He moved, excruciat-
ingly slowly, toward what he had started to think
of as light, but was really just a lighter shade of
darkness. He kept his arms twisted—his fingers
on the wall.

After about ten feet, Dom realized that the wall

was curving and the light was growing brighter. He thought he could almost make out the dark shape of the wall beside him. After twenty feet, Dom realized it wasn't a room at all. It was a tunnel.

Another five feet and the wall fell away from his fingers. He almost tripped at the suddenness of it. The wall he could just barely see sank back to form a small alcove. Dom stepped into the space and tried to see if it would lead to a door or another branch of the tunnel. The light, he soon realized, was coming from directly above his head. He looked up and saw what looked like a circle of pale light.

The alcove was only about a foot deep. At the back of the opening, Dom touched something that felt like a short metal bar. He tugged on it, thinking it might open a door, but it wouldn't move. Then he realized it wasn't just one metal bar but several spaced about a foot apart, vertically, on the wall. *What on earth?* Dom wondered, before it hit him.

It was a ladder.

Then Dom knew exactly where he was. The briny, saltwater smell . . . the cement tunnel . . . They (whoever *they* were) had tied him up in one of the bunkers. And, if Dom could just figure out how to climb a ladder with his hands tied behind his back, he might have just found a way out.

While Dom was considering if it was possible to go up a ladder backwards, he heard a shuffling sound from above his head. Someone was climbing down.

Dom hopped to the side. Was it Gregory? Was he coming back?

He waited. Dom didn't have a plan for when the person got to the bottom of the ladder. Without the use of his arms and legs, Dom was basically limited to some kind of body-slam wrestling move. Not that Dom knew how to wrestle.

He was still mulling his options over when his

potential captor reached the ground. The person was illuminated by the small halo of light. She turned and threw a hood back from her head.

It was Macy.

Chapter 16

It wasn't Macy.

Dom just wanted so desperately for it to be Macy that for one clear moment he saw her. But it wasn't Macy's hood, and the drawn, tired face definitely did not belong to Macy.

It was Julia.

"Hello Dominick," Julia said. She was holding what looked like a camping lantern. He could see a cut on her cheek, and the front of her hair looked singed, as if she had just been standing too close to a bonfire.

"What happened?" Dom asked. "And why am I tied up?"

"Which do you want to know first?" Julia asked. Her voice sounded flat, and she looked exhausted.

"Just untie me, okay?"

Dom waited while Julia sliced through the zip ties with a knife. She wasn't careful enough, and the blade nicked his wrist. It was a shallow cut, but it stung. When he was finally free, Dom shook out his legs and sort of flapped his arms until the blood started to flow to his fingers again. They were all pins and needles.

"Should I start talking or do you want to continue your exercises?" Julia remarked in what would have been sarcasm, but she looked too tired to even attempt a joke.

"What's going on? Where's Gregory?"

Julia gave him an appraising look. "Do you know what he did? Did you see?"

Dom nodded. "He killed some of them—your people—in the kitchen. And then he was feeding others to that crack in the bedroom. I saw Collins . . . his face was just . . . " Dom paused, not finding the words to express what he had seen. He didn't think the right words existed. "And then there was an explosion. I don't remember anything else."

"Gregory opened a Door," Julia explained. "The town is infested with ghosts."

"His name is Eli."

"What?" Julia had been looking down at her scarred hand, but then she glanced up at Dom like she hadn't understood what he said.

"You have to know that it wasn't Gregory doing those things. It was a ghost—the one that was inside our friend, Jackson. I don't know what happened, but the ghost, Eli, is inside Gregory now."

Julia nodded. "That explains it. It doesn't help, but it at least makes sense."

"Well?" Dom asked when Julia didn't start talking again. "What do we do?"

Julia still didn't talk, but gave him another one of her serious looks, like she was sizing him up.

"Anytime now," Dom said, growing impatient. He knew he was being rude, but she *had* tied him up and left him alone in a dark, creepy bunker.

Julia nodded as though she had just decided something. Or against something. "We start your lessons," she finally said. Then she turned around and started to climb back up the ladder.

Having literally nowhere else to go, Dom followed.

When Dom emerged on the top of the bunker (where men with huge, long-range guns used to guard the coast), he saw that it was morning. Just barely. The dim sky was tinged with yellow, and fog gathered along the beach. Dom couldn't see the land across the water, only more fog, so it looked like he was staring out at the open ocean rather than the Puget Sound. He felt adrift and wobbled as he took the last step off the ladder onto the cracked cement.

Tufts of grass sprouted from the cracks. Dom wondered how long until the bunkers were just a ruin, completely covered in green. How long, for that matter, until the whole town of Grey Hills just crumbled into the water? Dom thought about the end of humanity sometimes. Would it happen all at once—an asteroid or a nuclear war? Or would it happen little by little, person by person until no one was left.

Only ghosts.

"Come on," Julia said, leading the way down a sloping side of the cement structure. There were stairs instead of a ladder, which felt more civilized. Dom didn't realize exactly where they were until he saw the swing set. It had only been a few days since Dom had been here, but it felt like months. They were standing in the park where Sam and Jackson had found the second crack.

Dom and Julia walked down the steep embankment to the beach, and sure enough, there it was. The crack glowed an eerie blue beneath the waves. It was so bright, even in the morning light, that it resembled one of those rave glow sticks. But thinner, and frayed. The light seemed to bleed out from itself and curl and taper in every direction. The crack was growing.

"He'll be coming here next," Julia said. "We have to close it first."

"How did you know about this?" Dom asked.

"Gregory." Julia shook her head—not to deny anything, but maybe just because of the absurdity of it all. "Gregory told us. He told us everything that Sam told him. He always has."

"And now Eli has Gregory. Do you think he knows everything that Gregory knows? Is that what happens when a ghost . . . gets inside someone?"

Julia nodded. "He will have Gregory's memories. We have no secrets from Eli now. He'll know we're here. He probably knows exactly what I'm going to do next. But will he stop us in time? That is the question."

"To be or not to be," Dom muttered, then shook his head when Julia raised an eyebrow at him. "So, what's the plan? How are we going to close the crack? I didn't know you *could* close it."

"You can. It just isn't very . . . pleasant." Julia shivered. The sky was clear, Dom realized. Clear and cold. He could see their breath as they spoke. After so many days of rain and snow, a clear sky felt like hope.

It didn't take Julia long to find what they needed. The ghost was a girl. Young—maybe eight or nine years old. Or at least that was how old she was when she died. Who knows how many years she had been a ghost? Her dress looked like something one of Josie's old American Girl dolls used to wear, with a little white apron, and a bow tied at the back. The ghost had black hair, and she was looking right at them.

The girl started to walk toward them, limping. She frowned down at her leg, and then vanished—reappearing a few feet closer. She vanished again, and then was only about five feet away.

"Hello," the ghost said. "I'm Adeline." She gestured with her hand, but Dom wasn't sure what she was pointing to. Somewhere out toward the water. "I think my mom is a mermaid."

"What?" Dom said, his voice louder than he intended.

Adeline looked at him, flickering slightly when she turned her head. "What?" She frowned and pulled at her dark hair. Dom blinked, and Adeline was a few feet closer. "What?" she repeated.

Dom concentrated on Adeline—letting his mind grasp at her form. But this time, he didn't imagine her dissolving. Dom pictured holding the girl's body in his hand and keeping her there.

He imagined his hand closing tighter and tighter. "Adeline?" he asked, just to say something—to try and keep her calm. "Do you know where you are?"

The girl nodded her head, but then shook it, looking straight at Dom. "You're thinking about me. I don't want you to think about me. It hurts." She faded until Dom could see trees and the big cement forms of the bunkers behind her. Then she disappeared and reappeared right in front of him. "Stop it! Stop it! Stop it!" The ghost was screaming, with her hands over her ears. Her face was twisted into a terrifying scowl.

"Keep going," Julia said, nodding encouragingly. "That's right."

"But what am I doing to her?" Dom gasped. The ghost was screaming, and it was the most terrible sound he had ever heard. Then the girl was burning. It was just like those ghosts back in Texas—the Sirens. Whatever it was Gregory had done back then, Dom was doing now. And it felt like his whole head was splitting open.

Usually, when Dom took care of a ghost, it was just gone. Whatever power resided in the ghosts dissipated. But now, whatever Julia was having him do, was so different. If he was clenching the ghost in his closed fist, then she really didn't want to be held. This ghost kept screaming and screaming while Dom held out his hands toward her. Her skin was melting. Not burning, but actually melting like she was a doll made of wax who had been set too close to a flame.

"What the fuck did you make me do?" Dom demanded when it was over. There was no trace of Adeline. Dom felt unsteady, but also a little more solid at the same time. He could feel something uncurling inside of him—something strong.

When Julia spoke, her voice was calm, as if she was talking about the fucking weather. "This is how we're going to close the Doors. We can use them. We can use the ghosts' power. Instead of just dissolving them, we collect it."

Dom's lip curled. "This is sick. *Collect it?* Collect what? Their souls? What exactly are you doing to them?"

"What are *we* doing to them, I think you mean. They're dead, Dominick. It doesn't matter what happens to them. Are you going to tell me that you have been crying yourself to sleep at night over the hundreds of ghosts that you've 'taken care of' over the past few years? Ghosts that include your own sister?"

Dom sucked in his breath, glaring at her. "How do you know about that?"

"We know a lot of things about you, Dominick. I think we know just about everything."

Dom didn't know what to say.

"Destroying ghosts has always been easy for you, hasn't it?" Julia continued. "You didn't even need anyone to teach you. You could just do it."

That was true. Dom knew that taking care of

ghosts was always harder for Trev and Sam. It took more out of them—left them exhausted. But not Macy. It had been easy for her, too, Dom remembered. She might have been better at it than Dom—stronger. But he didn't say that to Julia. Instead, he whispered, "What we do shouldn't be easy."

"Maybe, maybe not. But is it for you to decide?"

"Do I have a choice?" he asked, looking to the patch of grass where Adeline had burned up.

"I think you might be strong enough to help us. Save us, even." Then Julia cocked her head—she was starting to remind him of a teacher he used to have at the boarding school. That teacher used to ask a question and then tilt her head and just let the silence unravel until someone would answer. "Do you want to have a choice?" she finally asked. "Or would it be easier if I took out my gun and made you do this? Would it help you sleep at night?"

She didn't take the gun from her holster, but Dom glanced at her hand and saw, as if for the first time, her missing fingers and her waxy, scarred skin.

"You need me because you can't do it, can you?" he finally said. Dom was starting to sweat, and he felt hot behind his eyes. "Whatever it is you just had me to that ghost, it does something to you, doesn't it? It hurts you."

Julia frowned and looked away. She brushed her white-streaked hair back behind her ear with her mangled hand.

"How old are you?" Dom asked, looking more closely at the lines on her face.

She didn't answer right away, then looked him right in the eye as though daring *him* to be the first one to look away. "I'm nineteen. And yes, this is what it did to me. This is what it does to everyone, eventually."

Dom took a deep breath, making himself see all of her. Her eyes flashed blue, then green. Then they stayed a deep, dark brown. "It's killing you, isn't it?" he asked.

Julia was the first to look away after all. She turned toward the water—toward the crack whose light still undulated beneath the waves. "I wasn't strong enough. Gregory might have been. It had the least . . . effect on him. But now he's been swallowed by a fucking ghost and the rest of them are dead. You're all we have left."

Dom stood next to Julia, watching the blue light. They didn't speak for a few minutes. Dom didn't know how he was supposed to feel with this new energy coursing through his body. He felt hot, and then freezing—like he had a fever. He felt a strange kind of focus, as though his body knew more than his mind did about this power he had stolen from a ghost. That was what scared him the most—it felt so natural.

He held out his hand and concentrated on the bones and tendons. He stared at his skin.

Julia saw what he was doing. "Picture the sun,"

she said softly, as though trying not to break his focus. "Imagine you are holding it in your hand. That is the language this power speaks. Heat and light. Creation and destruction."

In the cup of his hand, a small pinprick of light began to form. It spun like a small galaxy, gathering up more light and heat until he held what looked like a tiny star in his hand.

All at once the light fizzled out and Dom was left feeling bereft and famished. He'd heard Trev and Sam describe how hungry destroying ghosts always made them, but Dom had never experienced anything quite like it before.

Right now, however, Dom felt as if the star he had formed in his hand had made a black hole in his stomach.

Julia reached out to steady Dom before he even realized he needed steadying. "That was good," she said, nodding her head in approval. "Now we try again."

"And then what?" Dom asked, still watching

the blue light quiver and ripple in the water. It was almost hypnotizing. "How is this going to close that crack? How is it going to help us close the new Door Eli opened?"

"I think you know," Julia said. "You know what it takes to close a Door."

Dom nodded slowly. "A ritual . . . sacrifice. It took four deaths to close the last Door." He tried to blink away the image of Macy . . . of her blood soaking into the ground. "But that had nothing to do with ghosts. Whoever killed Macy . . . " Dom was no longer sure it was Eli who had killed her. Eli wanted to open the Doors, not close them. "Whoever killed her wasn't sacrificing ghosts. He killed people."

"The ghosts aren't the sacrifice, Dom. And it isn't just one Door. There are cracks forming all over Grey Hills. Eli is going to split this town wide open if we don't stop him."

"Then tell me, what do you want me to do?"

A small line appeared right between Julia's eyes. Besides that, her face looked perfectly calm when she said, "We're going to burn Grey Hills to the ground."

159

Chapter 17

As soon as they left the movie theater, Trev and Sam drove to the old mansion that was a few blocks from school. It was easy to overlook the huge, run-down house that used to belong to Principal Richard Grey. The iron fence effectively blocked the property from view, and the tall trees in the front yard took care of the rest.

After Principal Grey's death the house was sold, and, over the years, it had passed through many hands. There was currently a big For Sale sign on the gate outside. The sign itself looked old, too, and may very well have been hanging from the gate for years. Trev couldn't imagine how much money it would take to fix the old Grey mansion up to its former glory. Apparently too much to tempt buyers.

When Trev, Sam, and Dom first arrived in Grey Hills, the first thing they did was check out the house, peering through the fence. One summer night, the three of them had even gone inside—Sam picking the lock, of course. But they didn't find anything more than an old, and frankly, dangerous house. Trev's foot had gone through a floorboard, and after a huge spider had crawled into Dom's hair they were all pretty happy to leave.

It was a hell of a disappointment, though, because at the time they had next-to-no leads about what had caused the Grey Hills school fire in 1966. And if a creepy old mansion held no secrets, then what hope did they have of figuring out the mystery?

Sam, Trev remembered, had actually wanted to just leave Grey Hills after they didn't find any real evidence of a ritual. She thought it was just an accident, and had nothing to do with the Doors. *Sorry, sis. Looks like you can't be right every time.* Although, now, Trev was starting to wish that they had listened to Sam. Who knows where they would be now if they had just left Grey Hills before the school year even started. They had been talking about going to Wyoming next. Trev had always wanted to see some buffalo.

Trev parked next to the big gate. No one was around to see Sam pick the lock. No one living, at least. A few ghosts stood along the fence, looking lost. One of the ghosts, a man wearing only a bathrobe and his underwear, walked up behind Sam. He looked like he was trying to smell her hair. Before Trev had time to do anything besides call out Sam's name in warning, his sister spun around and jabbed her pick into the ghost's throat.

The man in the bathrobe made a sputtering sound. He looked surprised to Trev and raised a hand to his throat. Sam pulled out the pick, and the ghost vanished. Trev saw her wipe the pick on her jeans, even though there was nothing left of the ghost. Then she went back to work.

The grass in the front yard was withered, but still almost knee-high. Trev heard a rustling sound a few feet away. "What's that?" he whispered.

"Nothing." Sam shined the flashlight in the direction of the sound. A pair of yellow eyes caught the light. "A cat?"

"You sure?" Trev asked, walking faster.

"Maybe a raccoon? Jesus, Trev, I just stabbed a ghost and you're worried about a tiny furry animal?"

"They have teeth," Trev said, walking up to the front porch.

The front door was unlocked. Actually, it didn't appear even to be latched—the wood was so warped. He pushed, and the door swung open with a loud creek. The rustling in the grass resumed as whatever it was—cat, raccoon, small goblin— scampered away.

"Where do you think it is?" Trev asked, wishing he could turn on a light. The smell was terrible—kind of moldy and swampy. He put out a hand and touched spongy, rotting wallpaper. Trev snatched his hand back.

Sam pulled the collar of her shirt up over her mouth, probably to block out the smell. In a muffled voice, she replied, "Mabel said his brother kept Eli's body in the house. That he refused to bury him. Do you think it was a Norman Bates kind of a thing?"

"If he died in an explosion, then wouldn't his body be, you know, exploded? Would he even have a body left?" Trev had been wondering about that since they left the theater. In the movies, people were usually just little bloody bits after getting blown up.

"I don't know," Sam snapped. "I wasn't there." He looked back and could just make out a scowl plastered on his sister's face. She probably was hungry after taking care of that ghost back there. He would have offered her one of the three candy bars that he stole from the movie theater, but she was so *against* theft.

"Okay," Trev said. "Where do we look? Where would you be if you were a one hundred-year-old skeleton?"

"In a closet?"

It took Trev a moment to realize that Sam had made a joke. A lame one. "Couldn't Mabel have at least told us what floor to start with? Maybe a general wing?"

"To be honest, I don't think Mabel was all there."

"No shit," Trev said, "Although I think she has the right idea. If I was going to haunt a place it would definitely be somewhere fun. Maybe not a movie theater." He considered his options, watching Sam's beam of light catch cobwebs and the dust that their feet stirred up. "I think I would haunt Disneyland."

"Disneyland? Is that your final answer?"

"Definitely. I could go on all the rides without

waiting in line, and I could freak out children during the *It's a Small World After All* ride."

"I'm glad you have a plan, bro. Maybe you should start an afterlife career-counseling service. Help people get the most out of their hauntings." Sam led them through the kitchen, which looked like it hadn't been updated since the seventies. Everything was a disgusting yellow color.

Next, they walked through the living room, which was mostly empty except for a few moldering boxes of books. They looked in the hearth, but the only thing Trev saw was a rat. It twitched its nose at him and stood its ground. Brave little fuck.

It took them almost an hour to go through the entire house. After the first few rooms, Trev started to feel like they were being followed, but every time he turned around, the hall or bedroom or bathroom was empty. Sam said she didn't hear anything besides the creaking of the house itself, but Trev swore that, every few minutes, he could hear the scrape of a foot.

"I don't know," Sam said when they went back downstairs. "It has to be here somewhere." They had even checked the truly creepy attic, but only found a few toys—which, Trev was pretty sure, was part of the plot of every horror movie he'd ever seen. None of the toys came to life and stared at him with unblinking dolls' eyes, so Trev considered that a resounding success, even if they didn't find Eli's body or the journal.

"Does it?" Trev asked. "Is there really any reason why Mabel would tell us the truth?"

"It sounded true," Sam sighed. "Or maybe I just really wanted to believe her. She seemed so sad, you know?"

"And sad people can't be liars?" Trev looked up toward the tall ceilings. The broken windows had started to let in the morning light. He heard one of their stomachs rumble. Trev pulled out two candy bars from his secret stash. "Here," he said, handing one to Sam. "Don't judge."

She raised an eyebrow, but took the bar without a word. They ate the chocolate in silence.

What was their next move if they couldn't find the journal? Could they fight Eli without it? Trev tried to imagine what Eli would make Gregory do next. Would he go to the crack by the beach and open a new Door? Would he just sit back and bask in his new town of the dead that he had created? Did the ghosts know that it was Eli who had set them free? Was he their king now?

Trev was wadding up his candy-bar wrapper and was about to throw it at Sam's head when he heard a voice behind them.

"Are you giving up? That's a shame."

Trev and Sam both spun around—Sam dropped a third of her uneaten chocolate onto the ground. Standing before them was a boy about their own age. He had dark hair, and, even in the gloom of the old house, Trev could see that his eyes were a bright green. The boy was smiling broadly—his teeth catching the light from the windows.

He was clearly a ghost.

"Who are you?" Trev asked, his mouth sticky from the chocolate.

"Henry," the ghost said. "Henry Grey."

Trev was just thinking that Henry had totally pulled off the James Bond-shtick, when Sam's face turned murderous. She threw herself at the ghost.

Chapter 18

"Absolutely not!" Dom backed away from Julia, keeping an eye on the gun at her side. "Burning Grey Hills? That isn't . . . you can't do that."

"We have to." Her voice was still so fucking calm. She gestured out to the water and the glowing blue line. "These cracks that your friend opened? They're growing. They're all going to turn into Doors. He's started something that we can't stop—not without a great sacrifice. That's what the Doors want." She paused then, as though considering her next words. "They want death, Dominick. One way or another."

He shook his head. "You can't murder

thousands of people. There are whole families here—children. Why do you get to play God with their lives?"

"I'm not playing at anything," Julia said. "Do you think I like being the one who has to make this choice?"

"Then don't. There has to be another way."

"We've tried. For years we've tried to find another way than killing people to close the Doors. Nothing works."

Then don't close them, said a voice in the back of Dom's head. He had thought about that before, after tracking the Doors on the Map of the Dead. Did they have to be closed? Or were the Doors there for a reason? But the other Doors around the country were small—nothing like what had opened behind the school. If the Door Eli had opened in the yellow house was even bigger . . .

"Isn't there anything else we can do?" Dom asked again. He could hear the seagulls screaming in the distance and the soft plash of the waves. To fill this town with fire and watch it burn . . . that was unimaginable.

Julia's eyes went green, then hazel. He wondered how many ghosts were inside her—did she store them up like a battery? Dom could feel the energy coming off her, now that he knew what if felt like himself: it was almost a vibration—a spring wound too tight and about to burst. "There's no other way," she said. "But I can do it myself, if you won't help me."

"What can you do, Julia darling?"

Dom turned at the unmistakable sound of Gregory's low, almost raspy voice. Gregory was standing above them on the bank. He looked like a giant.

Julia's hand shot out at the sight of Gregory. A burst of light struck Gregory in the chest, and he was knocked backward and out of sight from the beach below.

"Shit," Julia hissed under her breath. She looked

to Dom. "We have to do it now, before he opens the crack."

"I don't know how," Dom said, but that wasn't exactly the truth. He could feel it—the power in his core. It flared up in his chest as he imagined fire blooming in his hands and spreading across the town. But it wasn't enough, the energy he'd stolen from that one ghost. Even if Dom was willing to do what Julia asked, it wouldn't be enough.

He looked around for more ghosts lingering beside the crack, but the beach was empty. "Where are the ghosts?" he said. "They're gone."

"Gregory. It must be him—they must flock to him now." As Julia spoke his name, Gregory reappeared above them as though summoned.

He hopped down the embankment and landed on the rocks and sand beside them. Gregory's eyes weren't just flickering from one color to the next—they were all colors at once. It hurt Dom's head to look at him, as though his brain couldn't process what he was seeing.

"You guys are making this far too easy for me." Gregory smiled at them. How had Dom not seen Eli inside Gregory before? It was unmistakable now. There was almost nothing left of Gregory in his face. "I was looking for you two. I was going to find you and bring you back here, but it turns out you've just been waiting for me all along."

Dom didn't realize he was backing up until the water was up to his knees. There was nowhere else to go unless he wanted to start swimming. He looked down, and the crack was only a few inches from his shoes. It pulled at him—at something inside him. It wanted to suck him dry.

Then, in one swift motion, Julia pressed something into Dom's hand. She had finally returned his phone. "Run," she instructed, giving him one last look. Her eyes were blue. Was he finally seeing her true eye color? And then she shoved Dom away and threw herself at Gregory. They fell together into the shallow water.

Light covered Julia and Gregory, and, for an

instant, Dom paused, transfixed by what he saw. The water around them started to froth and boil, and the light looked more like a flame licking at the tangle of limbs. Dom saw an arm start to blacken from the fire, and he had time to wonder whose flesh he was watching burn before he heard Julia screaming.

Dom turned and ran. He didn't look back, especially when the screaming stopped.

Dom ran back to the entrance to the bunker and threw himself down the ladder. He used his phone as a flashlight and sprinted down the long, cement corridor. There were tunnels connecting all the bunkers, Dom remembered. He had read that it went on for miles, twisting this way and that. A person could get lost in there.

He chose a door almost at random and slammed it closed behind him. There was no lock, but he held his hand over the thick metal handle and imagined a small star in the palm of his hand. At first, nothing happened, but then his hand grew so hot that his skin started to blister. The handle turned orange, and then sagged into itself and dripped into the floor.

Dom released the power and the heat was gone instantly. He blew on his aching hand, and once again remembered Julia's burned, mangled hand. Maybe he wasn't as special as she had thought. His skin seemed to burn just as easily as hers.

He pushed on the door, and it didn't move. Hopefully, that would keep Gregory out long enough for Dom to think of something.

Dom waved the light from the phone around the room. It was about ten feet by twenty and looked like a prison cell though it had probably been where the soldiers slept. He could see where bunk beds or cots might have lined the walls. There were no windows, and he couldn't see any other doors.

He leaned against a wall, and then sank to the ground. Looking at his phone, he saw with a deep, shuddering regret that there was no signal. "Shit," he whispered, and the mumbling echo of his voice bounced back to him, like the ghost of his past self.

Dom listened for footsteps, but didn't hear any. He emptied his pockets to see if there was anything useful—as if he could MacGyver a gun out of fucking pocket lint and loose change.

When he saw the plastic baggie that held Macy's unfinished Token sitting in his lap, along with his wallet and a few coins, he couldn't believe he had forgotten it was there.

Then it hit him: Blood. That's what Julia and Collins had said back in the graveyard. A Token needed blood from the living. Would his blood work? Could he finish the Token now?

The cut on his wrist from when Julia sliced through the zip ties wasn't deep and had already started to scab over. Dom picked at it with his thumbnail until a bead of fresh blood welled up. Then he dug his nail in deeper, until it was a trickle.

He opened the baggie and let his blood drip down onto Macy's Token. In the light from his phone, Dom couldn't see where it had soaked into the red ribbon. It looked exactly the same. *What now?* He wondered, holding the Token to his chest. Was there a magic word he was supposed to say? An incantation?

"Please," Dom whispered, closing his eyes. He tried to picture her face, but she kept turning away from him, her cape drifting out of the frame. "Macy, come back."

The phone had turned off while his eyes were closed, so when he opened them it was completely dark. He let out his breath and leaned his head back against the wall. It was stupid to think this would work. It was stupid to think he could bring her back.

Dom was about to throw the Token across the

room when he heard something. It sounded like fabric shifting, then sliding across the floor.

"Hello, Dominick."

It was Macy's voice.

Chapter 19

Sam's fists recognized the ghost before her brain remembered his name. She had seen Henry Grey's picture in old news articles about the Fire. His grinning face. And so she reacted before she could really think through what she was doing. Sam threw herself at Henry, trying to grab his neck, but her fingers passed right through him.

Henry stepped to the side, and Sam fell to the ground. "Not an auspicious beginning," he said, the smile gone from his face. "You could at least tell me your name before you try to kill me."

"You're already dead," she spat at him, scrambling to her feet. "And you killed Macy."

"What?" her brother exclaimed, and Sam remembered that she hadn't told her brother all of the things she had learned while she was on her Seattle holiday.

Sam gestured toward Henry. "He's the boy Jackson saw in the woods on Halloween. He killed Macy."

Henry held his hands out in front of him as though warding off her accusations. "I closed the Door. You should be thanking me."

Sam didn't want to hear another word from Henry Grey. She was just about to reach for Macy's knife so she could try to cut his mouth off of his face when Henry said, "You're looking for Eli's journal, aren't you?"

"Yes," Trev said a little too quickly, "You know where it is?"

"Don't tell him anything," Sam said to her brother, but she glanced at Henry to see what he would say next.

A smile returned to Henry's face. "I can take

you to it." When Henry had smiled a moment ago, Sam had thought it was a gloating smile. She thought he was mocking them. Now, however, his smile looked relieved. "I can help," Henry said. "If you let me."

Sam fingered the knife in her pocket, but she nodded. "Show us the journal, then we'll talk."

Henry led them to a small library or office. There was a large, wooden desk that looked like it would be a bitch to move—it seemed too large to fit through the door. Bookshelves with a few scattered, rotting books lining the walls.

"It's in here?" Trev asked. "Please don't tell me the journal was just sitting on a bookshelf all this time. Actually, do tell me that. That would be amazing."

Sam scanned the shelves with her flashlight, but none of the spines looked familiar.

Henry walked to the back of the office. He felt along the wall. "Interesting fact about this room," Henry said while he was tapping and pressing different parts of a shelf. "This used to be a nursery. My father slept in here when he was a baby." He must have found what he was looking for—a latch or a button—because half of the bookshelf swung away.

"My grandfather, Kenneth Grey, that is, made some improvements to this room when he converted it to his office." Henry stepped aside, and let Sam shine her light into the secret compartment. "There are all kinds of nooks and crannies in this room. I suppose my grandfather had plenty of secrets."

The opening sank back into the wall a few feet, and then there was what looked to be a set of closet doors. The handles had once been locked together with a rusty chain, but a few links were broken, and the two doors were open just a crack.

"What is it?" Trev asked. He was right behind

her shoulder, crowding her. Sam pulled on one of the handles, and the hinge groaned as it opened. Eli's skeleton grinned at her from the shadows.

Sam jumped back, running into Trev. "Holy hell!" she gasped, the light flickering in her unsteady hand.

There, somehow, clutched in Eli's bony arms, was the journal.

Henry spoke again. He was standing right behind Sam, and she once again resisted the urge to simply stab him in the face. "Eli didn't die in the explosion. That's what we were told. But when he was inside my head, I was also inside his. One hundred years ago, Eli tried to stop my grandfather from performing the ritual to keep the Door closed. Eli thought it was wrong to keep it closed. He thought that the Door was just going to keep growing hungrier and hungrier until it devoured the whole town. Eli wanted the ghosts in the Door to go free.

"My grandfather cut his brother's throat. He

told everyone that Eli died in the explosion because there were no witnesses to say otherwise."

"Jesus," Sam said, looking at the skeleton's tilted head. She reached in and pulled at the journal. At first it wouldn't come away, but then Eli's arm fell off, releasing the book.

"Fuck, Sam," Trev exclaimed. "Did you have to do that?" He put his sleeve over his mouth, even though there wasn't really a smell from the bones themselves. At least, Sam didn't think there was. She had been holding her breath.

"Okay, we have the journal," Sam said, dismissing Henry's sob story about Eli. She didn't give a fuck how Eli died. She just wanted him to die a second time and stay dead. "We have to destroy it, right?"

"You have to take it to him," said Henry. "He needs to be there when you burn it."

Sam didn't stop to ask why. It wasn't as if she could fact-check what this ghost was telling her. Henry had helped them find the journal—she'd just have to trust him one more time. "We don't know where he is," Sam said. The journal was cold in her hands, like holding a dead thing.

Henry grinned at her, and for the first time since she saw him, it didn't make her want to rip off his jaw. "I'll take you to him."

Chapter 20

Dom fumbled with his phone, finally managing to turn on the light.

Macy stood before him. She was still wearing her Halloween costume, with the gray dress and red cape. Her hood was up, so her face was hidden in its shadows. Dom remembered the way Macy's cape had dragged on the ground when Sam and Trev carried her through the woods. He also remembered how, when she kissed him, the fabric of the cape had felt so smooth against his hands that it was almost like trying to hold onto water—like Macy was something that was made to slip through his fingers.

"Macy?" Dom's voice cracked. "Is that really you?"

"I don't know how to answer that." Her voice was so soft that he felt like he should be straining to hear it, but at the same time it was everywhere. She was the rain and the wind. She filled his mind. "I'm not who I was, but yes, I think I'm still me. At least, I remember being me, so that must count for something."

"Are you . . . I mean, can I touch you?" He swallowed. Dom couldn't find the right words. He could never say the right things when she was alive, so why should it be any different now?

Macy laughed. She threw back her hood and underneath he saw that she was exactly as he remembered her. There was no blood staining her dress, no horrible line across her throat. And her eyes—they looked alive. "I don't know. Should we find out?"

Dom blinked and Macy was in front of him,

just inches away. He gasped and leaned back. She frowned.

"I didn't meant to scare you."

"I'm not scared," Dom whispered, willing himself not to be.

She shook her head. "You are scared. I can hear your heart. I can almost see it pounding in your chest. Do you think I'll hurt you? Do you really think that?"

Dom started to say that no, no, he would never think that. She would never hurt him. But then he met her eyes and knew that he didn't want to lie to her. He told the exact truth. "I don't care."

"Oh, Dom," Macy's eyes were sad, and she looked down at her hands. "That's not a good answer."

"Why did you wait so long to come back?" He didn't say, *Why did you wait until I finished the Token? Until I made you come here?*

Macy looked up, meeting his eyes again. She smiled, but it didn't feel like a smile. He thought it was the look someone gave you when they were trying to find a way to say goodbye. "It hurt more than I thought it would."

Dom's eyes widened in horror. "Do you mean . . . " his mouth went dry. "Did it hurt? When you died?"

She took another step forward and rested her hand on his shoulder. Where she touched him began to tingle, but he wasn't sure if that was because she was a ghost or because she was Macy.

"No. I didn't know that *this* would hurt so much. Seeing you. I just . . . I thought it might rip me apart if I tried."

Dom lifted his hand toward her, then hesitated—leaving his hand an inch from Macy's cheek. He cupped the air around her. She flinched, and he lowered his hand.

"I'm sorry," she said. He still wasn't sure if he was hearing her voice, or if it was echoing through the inside of his head. "I just . . . you aren't going to, you know? *Take care* of me?"

"No," Dom began, but then he made himself stop. Again, he told her the truth. "I thought about it. I thought about this over and over. What would I do if I saw you again. What *should* I do?"

"Well?" Macy asked in her strange, soft voice. "What *should* you do?"

His hand was still hovering near her face. She watched him with her jaw set, as if she didn't know what he was going to do next and was bracing herself. The thing was, Dom didn't know either. He thought of all the words he had meant to tell her, but they fell away.

Dom remembered when he destroyed his sister and how she had looked so surprised. Macy wouldn't be surprised. She was expecting it. "You don't have to stay," he whispered, his voice unsteady. "If that thing I made—that Token—is keeping you here, if I'm controlling you . . . I don't want to control you."

"I know," she said, but her smile was gone. "We never mean to make our chains."

Dom had no words. He never had, not really. Even when Macy was alive he never knew what to say to her. He had never told her how he felt.

Slowly, he brought his hand closer to her face. She didn't flinch this time, but kept her eyes on his. *Your eyes are a forest*, he might have said, *and I'll never find my way out of them*. But still, he didn't speak.

When his palm touched her, she closed her eyes and leaned into his hand. He thought he could feel the tears on her face. She felt like a dream that is so real you almost don't know the difference. When you wake up, you can tell—you know that the contours of the dream (the texture, the details) were not clear enough. Something was missing. But Dom wanted to stay in this dream. He wanted to forget that Macy was once *more* than this ghost standing before him. He wanted to believe that she was whole, one more time.

When he kissed her, he thought he could taste

her sorrow, like nettles, and her anger like a bitter medicine.

When she kissed him back, she tasted like rain.

Eli found him moments later. He pounded on the metal door. "Come on out, Dominick. Your turn."

Dom stood up. The light from the phone was just enough so he could see the fear on Macy's face. "I won't let him hurt you," Dom whispered.

"Oh, Dom." Macy put her hood back up over her head, "No one can hurt me." Then she walked through the door.

Chapter 21

As Sam climbed down the ladder into the bunker, she wondered again why she was blindly following a ghost who had murdered their friend. But Henry hated Eli, so maybe that old saying was true: the enemy of my enemy is my friend. Sam needed Henry to be on their side. She needed all the help she could get if they were going to destroy Eli.

Sam helped Trev off the ladder and then got out the flashlight. The darkness seemed to absorb the light, funneling it down to a narrow beam. She heard voices in the distance. Sam froze for a moment, trying to imagine what they were going to find, but Trev was pulling on her arm.

"Come on," he said. "There's no time."

As they ran down the tunnel, Sam realized she didn't know where Henry had gone.

The metal door began to glow, and then Dom leapt aside as it burst inward. A piece of broken metal skimmed Dom's forehead and blood ran into his eyes. He looked up, and Gregory was standing in the broken doorway. He was glowing a bluish light that was tinged with green.

Dom reached into himself and felt for the store of energy he had taken from Adeline's ghost. There was a spark left, but it fizzled and died as he reached for it. He felt hollowed out, as though Adeline's power had consumed something inside of him and now he was empty.

Eli—inside Gregory—laughed. "The Wardens had such high hopes for you, Dominick. They said you were so powerful. But here you are, about to die like everyone else." Eli walked forward, his arms held out. Was Dom going to burn with his face pressed to that crack like Collins? Or was Eli just going to rip his heart out right here? Was Eli going to paint the walls with Dom's blood like he had done to the Wardens in the kitchen?

When he was only inches from where Dom sat crouched and bleeding on the cold floor, Eli stopped, and turned around. "You?" Eli asked, laughing again.

Then Eli left the room, and Dom was plunged back into darkness.

Sam held the journal out in front of her like it was a shield. "Stop!" she cried, as Gregory came toward them. "Stop right now."

"Oh Sam, do you think you can use that against me?" A bluish, greenish light flickered over his face.

Gregory looked like he was burning. "*I* made the Token. Only *I* can use it."

Then he backhanded Sam, and her barely healed lip split back open. As Gregory picked up the journal that had fallen out of her hands, she screamed in frustration. All this work, and he had the journal back?

Sam got to her feet, pushing past Trev who was trying to help her up. She took Macy's knife out of her pocket and flicked her wrist. The blade caught the strange light. Sam was about to throw it at Gregory's head when she saw someone step out of the darkness behind him.

Macy walked up to Gregory and sank her hand into his back. Sam didn't know what Macy was doing—maybe grabbing his spine or his heart. For an instant, Gregory stopped, dropping the journal. Then a light shot out from him, and Macy's ghost vanished.

While Gregory was distracted, Sam drew back her arm and flung the knife. It flew lower than she was aiming and lodged itself in Gregory's chest. Gregory fell back.

Behind her, Sam heard Trev cry out.

I'm sorry, Sam thought as she caught her brother before he could run past her. She held him until he sank to his knees in sobs.

When Gregory stood back up, Sam kept her arms around Trev—protecting her brother with her body. If she couldn't stop Gregory, then she would at least slow him down.

Dom stepped out of the room and saw Sam's knife strike Gregory.

Dom ran toward them, not sure what he could do, but knowing he had to do something. Then Macy was at his side. She pulled him back. "Use me," she said. "Use me to save them. Take me and use my power to destroy the journal."

"No." Dom shook his head. "You don't know what it does."

Macy grabbed his face and made him look at her. "I know exactly what will happen, and I want you to do it. If you don't, Eli is going to kill them. There's no time."

"No," he said again. "I won't let you."

"It's not your choice."

"Yes, it is." Dom reached into his pocket and pulled out her Token. "I can tell you *No*, and you have to listen."

Macy knocked the Token out of his hand. "Do you really think that's why I came back? It never worked, Dom. You never knew how to make a fucking Token. Jesus. I came back because I love you. And now you are going to save our friends."

Macy placed her hand on Dom's chest. Then her hand sank in. He couldn't breathe. "Do it," she said. "Do it now or you'll die too."

Dom tried to resist, but she was squeezing his heart. His mind reached out without his permission.

It took hold and began to close around her like a vice. Tears filled her eyes, and he could see that she was in pain.

"I thought nothing could hurt you," he whispered, his own tears blinding him.

She loosened her grip ever so slightly. "Only you," Macy said. Then she began to scream.

Dom tried to stop. He could feel himself starting to absorb her. She had so much more power than Adeline. She had always been so much *more* . . .

Then Macy was ripped out of Dom's grasp. A boy with black hair was standing in her place. Dom cried out, and his hands automatically reached for Macy. The boy moved to block him. "No." the stranger said. "Not her. Use me instead." The ghost took Dom's hands and placed them on either side of his head.

His green eyes were all Dom could see. "Do it," the ghost said. "Before Eli kills them, too." This time Dom didn't hesitate. As the ghost melted, he didn't make a sound. Dom thought the ghost was smiling.

Dom felt like he could fly. The green-eyed ghost had lit the white-hot center of a sun inside Dom's chest. He could do anything.

He glanced to where Macy had fallen, but she was gone. Then he ran the rest of the way to Gregory. Eli was holding his journal again, and he laughed when he saw Dom. "Come to watch as I rip their heads off?" he asked. "Or maybe I'll keep them alive until you've helped me open the next Door. Do you think they'd like to watch your face burn? Sam might . . . "

Dom nodded. He knew Sam could hear him when he said, "Yeah. But I've always been kind of an asshole." Then Dom reached out, and, focusing on the journal in Gregory's hands, he imagined it burning. And not only the journal—he pictured the ghost who was crouched inside Gregory burning as well. He thought of Eli's bones cracking, and his skin peeling. Dom burned Eli in his mind until he was nothing but cinders.

Dom hadn't realized he had closed his eyes until he heard the sound of someone falling to the ground. He heard the loud crack of a head hitting the cement. Dom opened his eyes and saw Sam holding a flashlight for Trev, who was crouched over Gregory.

"Did it work?" Dom whispered, before he sank to the ground himself. A cool hand caught his arm. Macy's hand.

"Yes," Macy whispered. "Eli's gone."

Chapter 22

Sometime in the early morning, Claire woke up.

It was still dark out when Sabrina had fallen asleep in Claire's arms. At the time, Claire was so tired that her head kept drooping down so her chin touched her chest, but then she would snap her head back up. She couldn't fall asleep with a ghost in her sister's room. Not even if it was Nick.

At least, that's what she had thought, but when she opened her eyes she knew from the light coming in the window that hours must have passed. Beenie was back in her bed, and Claire was curled up on the floor with a blanket draped over her. She sat up and looked around the room.

There, sitting in a chair across the room, was Nick. She could see him. She could see his ghost.

"Hi," Nick said, almost shyly. "Macy wanted me to say hi if I saw you."

Claire could barely feel the tears the streamed down her face. All she could see was him. Macy had described how Nick looked after the accident, but he didn't look that way here.

He looked perfect.

Chapter 23

Trev was still down in the bunker with Gregory's body, so it was just Sam, Dom, and Macy who stood at the top, looking down on the new Door. It wasn't as big as the one Eli had opened in the yellow house, but it looked like it was still growing.

Some of the ghosts vanished once they stepped from the Door onto the beach. Others stood around with dazed expressions. One ghost, a child, started to laugh. Another began to scream.

It was Sam who spoke first. "What are we going to do?"

Dom closed his eyes. Henry's power was still humming in his blood, and, for a moment, he could sense the Doors—and all of the cracks that would eventually become Doors themselves. They pulsed brightly in the map of his mind, ripping wider like seams about to burst. He thought about what Julia had told him before she died. Dom could close the Doors if he wanted. He could burn Grey Hills to the ground.

He opened his eyes and answered Sam's question. "I don't know."

Macy stood beside him. In the morning light, her body wasn't completely solid. Through her, he could see the distant curve of the beach, and the flash of the lighthouse pulsed somewhere in her neck. She took his hand, and together they watched the ghosts—like survivors from a distant shipwreck—pull themselves onto the shore.